Danny Hill
Memoirs of a
Prominent Gentleman

Danny Hill
Memoirs of a
Prominent Gentleman

EDITED WITH AN INTRODUCTION BY
FRANCIS KING

First published in 1977 by Hutchinson & Company
This edition published in 1987 by GMP Publishers Ltd
P O Box 247, London N15 6RW

Distributed in the United States of America by
Subterranean Company
P 0 Box 10233
Eugene
Oregon 97440
USA

British Library Cataloguing in Publication Data

King, Francis, 1923–
    Danny Hill: memoirs of a prominent gentleman.
    I. Title
    823′.914[F]   PR6061.I45

    ISBN 0-85449-058-2

Printed by the Guernsey Press, Guernsey, C.I.

INTRODUCTION

The manner in which this sequel to John Cleland's *Memoirs of a Woman of Pleasure* came into my possession is a curious one. When I was working for the British Council in Japan in the late fifties and early sixties, a frequent and welcome attender at our lectures and a no less frequent but rather less welcome caller at my house was an elderly Australian, Thomas Wainewright. Apparently without any relations or close attachments, he had chosen Kyoto as his improbable place of retirement after a life of sheep-farming. He had written a great deal but had published nothing; and now, in his late seventies, he was still indefatigably pouring out poems, short stories, plays and novels. Learning that I was a writer, he would often leave with me a wad of manuscript. The cheap paper was always lined but he took no notice of this, his large, sloping, unformed handwriting rarely managing to get more than a hundred words on to a sheet. Because I suffer from a sense of duty, because I felt sorry for the old boy and because I rather liked him, I used to force myself to skim through each of his offerings and then try to make comments that were neither so untruthful as to offend my conscience nor so truthful as to offend him. A difficult task. After I left Japan, he continued from time to time to write to me and to send me examples of his work. Increasingly I delayed in answering him and when, at long last, our correspondence petered out, I must confess that I felt more relieved than sorry.

Some years later, in 1974, I received a letter from a solicitor in Alice Springs to tell me that my Australian friend had died – not in Kyoto, but in an old people's home back in his native country, where he had been lying semi-paralysed for several months – and that he had willed to me not only a small sum of money but also all his literary manuscripts. I was far from eager to receive the second of these bequests but the solicitor put forward the perfectly reasonable opinion that I could hardly accept the one without accepting the other. Eventually a huge, battered tin trunk, which used to fill most of the tiny room that the Australian occupied in his Japanese lodging house, turned up to fill most of my study. I began to go through its contents at first conscientiously and then with increasing boredom, irritation and speed, dumping each manuscript as I finished it into one of a number of plastic bags destined for the dustman. At the bottom of the trunk I at last came on a square box, made of mahogany with brass corners. A tattered label, stuck to the lid, merely read 'A Prominent Gentleman'. When I looked inside, I found this book – which, as I started to decipher its faded handwriting, interested me far more than the manuscripts through which I had previously been riffling.

Naturally I wondered how the book had come into the possession of someone as improbable as my Australian friend; and I also wondered whether it was the work of John Cleland himself or of a later hand. The solicitor, who had evidently never heard of Cleland, could give me no assistance and could provide no names of relatives or antecedents of my benefactor. The remainder of his estate, which was predictably small, had been left to the Japanese woman whom I had always assumed to be only his landlady but whom I now, in retrospect, saw in a different light.

It was only as I was typing out the manuscript that I suddenly saw a possible link between my old friend and Cleland. It will be remembered that, having left Bombay in disgrace and having, on his return to England, served more than one prison sentence for debt, in 1747 Cleland sold his manuscript of *Memoirs of a Woman of Pleasure* to

6

one Ralph Griffiths, a bookseller, for twenty guineas. Griffiths subsequently made some ten thousand pounds out of the book and was thus enabled to fulfil the dream of every publisher: to live the life of a gentleman. Griffiths had a daughter Anne by a second marriage, who eventually married a Thomas Wainewright and had by him a son, also baptized Thomas. This Thomas Wainewright is the subject of an entertaining essay by Oscar Wilde, called *Pen, Pencil and Poison* (1899). With ambitions both to be an artist and to live the gentleman's life of his grandfather, the young Thomas took to an occupation almost as reprehensible as his grandfather's exploitation of starving authors – the wholesale poisoning of his relatives. (When asked why he had done away with his young sister-in-law, Helen Abercromby, he replied airily that he had not been able to abide the thickness of her ankles.) Eventually 'kind, light-hearted Wainewright' – as Charles Lamb described him – was transported to Van Diemen's Land, where he died after a few years. Whether, as the identical name suggests, he was an ancestor of my friend and whether he took into his enforced exile a manuscript either bequeathed to him by his grandfather or stolen from the uncle whom he murdered, must remain in doubt. But I should like to think that both such links exist.

In dismissing the action of the Corporation Counsel of New York, together with the five District Attorneys of the five counties that make up New York City, to suppress the American publication of the *Memoirs*, Supreme Court Justice Arthur G. Klein said in the course of his opinion: 'While the saga of Fanny Hill will undoubtedly never replace Little Red Riding Hood as a popular bedtime story, it is quite possible that were Fanny to be transposed from her mid-eighteenth-century Georgian surroundings to our present-day society, she might conceivably encounter many things which would cause her to blush.' But were she able to read these memoirs of her brother, I feel sure that all that might make her blush would be his incidental revelations of her own early career.

7

In his introduction to the French translation of *Memoirs of a Lady of Pleasure (L'Œuvre de John Cleland*, Bibliothèque des Curieux 1914), Guillaume Apollinaire wrote of the book: '*Le seul ouvrage qui garde de l'oubli le nom de John Cleland, c'est le roman de Fanny Hill, la sœur anglaise de Manon Lescaut, mais moins malheureuse, et le livre où elle paraît à la saveur voluptueuse des récits que faisait Chéhérazade.*' I should like to think that this sequel also has something of that '*saveur voluptueuse*' and that it may assist in keeping the memory of John Cleland fresh long after that of his publisher has vanished into oblivion.

FRANCIS KING

DANNY HILL

*Memoirs of a Prominent
Gentleman*

Before, a joy propos'd; behind, a Dream.
SHAKESPEARE, *Sonnets*, 129

I

When I was born, the village midwife (a woman who, in her mature years, used her big mouth with the same bawdry as, in her prime, she had used an even larger orifice) proclaimed as she dandled me in her arms, all puckered and puling, that there was little doubt that I should one day become a gentleman of great prominence. In this forecast she was proved to be right by such subsequent events as I shall in due course relate in this narrative: I have always had a head start on all other comers in the Stakes of Cupid. The midwife indulged in sundry other sallies, to the effect that in her day she had known many fine, upstanding gallants but that this was the first time that she had ever delivered such a fine, upstanding brat; that she had been momentarily afeared that my mother had been taken to bed of a tripod instead of a biped; and that the old saying that one should never send a boy to do the work of a man obviously did not hold good in such a remarkable case as mine.

The attribute which caused the good midwife so much amaze and glee I inherited, together with my raven hair, flashing eyes, white teeth, goodly features and stalwart build from the holy Cardinal P———, many years later to become the even more Holy Father, Pope———. The Cardinal had come on a visit to England and since my mother's employers, the elderly Duke of A——— and his youthful Duchess, were of the Old Faith, he had been lavishly entertained by them at their Castle. But among the feasts, the solemnities and the progresses, they had omitted one item for his proper care. This it was the fate of my poor mother, then an innocent girl apprenticed to her uncle the cook, to make good for him. She had been despatched to the gooseberry bushes to ascertain whether the fruit were yet ripe for the making of a sorbet of a kind for which my great-uncle was particularly famed when lo! like Zeus appearing in the guise of an eagle to Ganymede, the prelate swished down on her, in the course of one of his matutinal and meditational walks through the grounds of the castle. My mother, aghast that her skirt should be hitched so high and that her kerchief should be askew, knelt down, as she had been instructed to do, at the Cardinal's feet, her eyes downcast, to ask him for a blessing. But what was extended to her was, to her astonishment, far more knobbly than any episcopal ring. His Grace touched her chin and tilted her face up towards him. 'My child,' he said to her in his mellifluous English, 'do not be afeared. God's Creation is beautiful in all its parts and how can we best worship Him other than by enjoying each of those parts in turn?' He raised her to her feet and soon began toying with her breasts, then two hard, firm rising hillocks that had only but recently begun to show themselves. My mother, as yet totally insensible of the wiles of men and unable to believe that any ill could come of a personage of such reverence and distinction, suffered his touch; but this touch soon become like a lambent fire coursing over her whole body and thawing all coldness as it went. It was only when his hand slipped down yet lower, towards the soft silky down that had but a few months before put forth and now garnished the mount-pleasant of her body, that she attempted to pull free of him, begging him to unhand her. But the fire that his lascivious touches had lighted up still wantoned through all her veins and it was therefore with as much disappointment as relief that she saw that the old gardener was approaching. At that, the importunate prelate at once readjusted his robes, raised in a blessing the hand that had but recently been intent to probe her unbroken passage and passed on. Thus it was that the common superstition that babies are to be found under gooseberry bushes proved, in part at least, true in my case.

That night, as five of the other skivvies lay humped and snoring mightily in the attic bedroom that she shared with them under the eaves, my mother again bethought herself of the god-like prelate, of that singular and aberrant protrusion from between the folds of his robes and of the teasing torment of his hands. She tossed about on her bed, spread her thighs abroad and herself felt what she was now assured must be the gates to Paradise. Thus burning and fretting, in expectation of a longed-for relief that never came, she eventually fell into a sleep crowded with dreams at once portentous and titillating. Only the prelate, it was born in on her, could reduce her rebellious disorder.

But the next day and the day after that she saw nothing of him, even though, at any of her free moments (there were but few) she made some excuse to wander down into the vegetable gardens and skulk within the fruit-cages. There she received many a prick to her white, virgin flesh, but not such a prick as that for which she was searching so forlornly. On the third day, however, the eagle again descended; but instead of at once gathering her up with his claws to the seventh heaven of delight, he instead enjoined on her, 'Extreme secrecy is essential, otherwise Lord only knows what her Grace will have to say to me.' My mother was a little puzzled as to why he should be more concerned for the censure of the Duchess than for that of the Duke but she at once vowed that not even the extremities of the torturer's art would ever wrest from her any betrayal. The Cardinal then ascertained from her that it was one of her duties to rise betimes, long before dawn, to light the huge fire in the kitchen and told her that he would join her there. He arrived in a costly night-robe that put to shame my mother's simple, much-mended attire, and it was there, in front of the blazing fire, the tinder scattered all around her and her petticoat crammed into her mouth to stop her screaming, that my mother suffered that breach from my father's monstrous engine that eventually effected a passage for my emergence into the world. Having stuffed her virgin purse to overflowing with one commodity, the Cardinal then stuffed her bosom less liberally with some coins of the realm, before making wing to his own apartment. My mother was never to clap eyes on him again, since on the same day that had dawned on her shame the stealthy cropper of her virginity made his prudently premature departure for his native land. That my mother should have hit on the name of Daniel for me was due to the proximity of the fiery furnace at this hour of her undoing.

For lack of the Cardinal, my mother began to peak and pine; worse, as far as her employers and her superiors in the kitchen were concerned, she no longer now fulfilled her duties with the same alacrity and skill. As she peeled a mushroom for some masterpiece of the culinary art, she would dream, struggling with an overmastering faintness, of that column of ivory, beautifully streaked with blue veins and carrying, fully uncapt, a head of the liveliest vermilion; as she whipped the eggs for a syllabub, she would feel again those nuggets, nestling in their purse, that hung on to the root of their first instrument and minister. Frequently her uncle would ask what that dratted girl might be dreaming about; no less frequently the housekeeper would intimate that she might soon find herself out of a place and back in the family hovel with eight other brats, a goat, a couple of pigs and a mangy cur. My mother spurned all food in the days immediately after the departure of her dear undoer; but soon it did not escape her notice that, whereas in every other particular she was growing thinner and thinner, her belly was growing more and more protuberant. Finally it was evident both to the other members of the servants' hall and to herself that she was big with child.

The Duchess, apprised of the fact, summoned her errant servant to her, showing more curiosity in this matter than might have been expected of one of her

14

station in regard to someone so menial. Perhaps, being herself childless, she was therefore that much the more interested in ascertaining by what process conception had taken place. But my mother, faithful to her vow, refused to enlighten her, other than to say that she had been taken unawares while picking fruit in the garden; that she had been struck dumb by the violence of her surprise and had had neither the power to cry out nor the strength to escape from her ravisher's strenuous embraces; that she had taken no cognizance of his face; and that shame had prevented her from speaking of the matter to anyone subsequently. So far from this reticence satisfying the Duchess, it only provoked her to further and yet more insistent questioning. Was it the head-gardener, she demanded, who, though now advanced in years, was reputed to be still replete with all the genial juices of youth? Was it the idiot boy, who brought up the eggs from the farm and himself, so gossip had it, was the possessor of a couple of eggs that would do credit to an ostrich? Was it the estate carpenter, who had lost his position with a neighbouring grandee because of his skill in prising open the soft oiled wards of the female staff with his picklock. To all such inquisition my mother could only answer steadfastly, 'I do not know, ma'am, to be sure. I had never set eyes on him before, nor have I set eyes on him since.' Was his hair red? then demanded her Grace, no doubt thinking of the young priest who chanted so prettily through his nose in the family chapel; to which my mother replied, with an artfulness not usual to her, that she did not know, since her ravisher had kept his cap on. The Duchess was plainly exasperated at being fobbed off in this fashion; but, with unusual kindness, she told my mother that, provided the bastard were farmed out, she might retain her position after the birth. Whether this leniency was due to the fact that my mother had such a light hand with pastry or to the Duchess's hope eventually to plumb her secret, I can only speculate.

Before I was despatched to the good people who

brought me up in a neighbouring village, in total ignorance of my true origins, the Duchess demanded that I be shown to her. I was brought up to her chamber in my grieving mother's arms, while the Duke was out at the hunt, and the Duchess stooped over above me. Then she cried out and fainted clean away. When – her personal maid having burnt feathers under her nose and administered some hartshorn – she eventually recovered consciousness, she at once demanded that I should be stripped of my swaddling clothes. She stared; she put out a delicate hand as though to touch and then restrained herself; and finally she turned and began to upbraid my terrified mother. 'Wicked, wicked girl! You have told lies to me. It is clear beyond any shadow of doubt who was the author of your undoing; and it is equally clear that you yourself provoked that undoing by nefarious conduct. Tell me everything, child! Hide nothing from me, if you do not wish to be cast out into the highway!' Sobbing and wringing her hands, myself naked upon her knees, my mother now poured out the truth, while the Duchess, who had despatched her maid from the room, exclaimed, 'Lawks!' and, 'Wicked, wicked girl!' when not asking to be apprised of exact degrees of longitude and of exact measures of balsamic fluid. 'I had always guessed,' she confided 'that that august prince of the Church had more in him than at first meets the eye. Indeed, I once concealed myself and managed to espy, through a chink in the privy. . . .' She broke off, realizing the unsuitability of someone of her lineage speaking of such matters to a mere chit of a country wench. Not long after all this (I had by then been abstracted from my mother) Her Grace took herself off on a pilgrimage to Rome, leaving His Grace behind her, since he was by then too infirm, both from years, a love of the bottle and the inroads of the pox, to support a lengthy journey. Her purpose, so she said, was to implore the Cardinal to intercede on her behalf for an issue; and such was the devotion to which she applied herself to this task that twins, a boy and girl, were born, prematurely it was put about, shortly before the death of her spouse. Of this boy it was said that the word 'yard' was, for once, an apt one when used by country folk to describe what is the source both of the greatest pleasures and the greatest pains known to womenkind.

All that I have recounted so far, I learned many years later from my mother. In what circumstances I eventually refound her, I shall tell at a later stage in my narrative.

The goodly couple who took me in were a farmer and his wife, to whom my mother handed over the small supply of coins furnished by the prelate, together with myself. Both were now in their middle years and the wife had assumed that the powers of procreation had dried up within her, since her only two children, a son and a daughter, had been born some eighteen and nineteen years before. (Of this daughter, who had abandoned the house ere ever I had reached it, I shall write more anon.) Much to her amaze and delight, my foster-mother had found one day that, like my mother's, her belly was growing monstrous big and that she was afflicted with an inordinate craving for garlic, the roots of which she chewed incessantly, to the distress of her husband. She was eventually delivered of a puny female infant at about the same time as my mother; but though it was cosseted and pampered, it soon succumbed to some kind of quaternary fever, leaving its aging mother in a state of disconsolation, the cradle empty and her vast breasts aching from their overflowing burden of milk. She seized on me with delight when I was offered to her, remarking on the beauty of my features, the clarity of my complexion, and the perfection of my hands and feet. That, unlike the midwife, she did not comment on my most important attribute, was no doubt due to the innate modesty of this excellent woman; she certainly cannot have failed to remark on it.

With these people I spent the first fifteen years of my life, helping in the fields and with the care of the beasts, and studying, when I could find both time and opportunity, with the parson, who befriended me in my seventh year. This elderly gentlemen, with his shaggy white eye-brows, his abundant beard and his sagging dewlaps, had been destined, so I was told, for great preferment, being a noteworthy scholar and, more important, the brother of an Earl. But some obscure scandal, of which I never learned the truth, had caused his relegation to this tiny, remote village, in a reversal of fortune that my father, whether because of his greater cunning, the greater tolerance of his Church or some difference in his appetites, had been able to avoid with such success.

My encounter with the parson came about when, on an autumn day, I was engaged in the country pursuit of scrumping with two or three of my fellows, boys of the same age as myself but not of the same natural endow-ments. We were in the vicarage orchard and I was high in one of the apple-trees, biting on a juicy apple, when I heard bellows of rage, shouts of alarm and the patter of feet on the dusty pathway on the other side of the wall. I shinned down the tree as fast as I was able, grazing palms and knees, in order to effect my escape; but a gnarled hand gripped me by the seat of my trousers even as I was descending and a voice demanded: 'Boy! Boy! What are you doing here, boy? No, boy! You shall not evade me!'

I had been struggling so violently that my ancient trousers, once the property of the son of my foster-parents, suddenly split, revealing the snowy perfection of my posterior globes. I thought that I could now escape my persecutor but the gnarled hand, seeking for something to grasp me by, closed on my most prominent feature and brought me to a halt. 'Oh, sir, please sir!' I began to sob piteously, thinking of the shame that I should bring on the good people who had given me a home if I were to be handed over to the rigour of the law.

'Now, boy, stop that caterwauling! Do you not know the Ten Commandments?'

'Oh, yes, sir, indeed, sir!' I had been attending the Sunday School and I was surprised that the vicar did not know this, even though he left the major part of his duties to his curate.

'Thou shall not steal, boy!'

'Yes, sir! Ow, sir!' (At this point he had given me an unmannerly tug.) 'Please, sir!' I began to explain, with some slight exaggeration pardonable in my predicament, how the droughts of the early summer and the subsequent tempests had reduced my foster-father to a state of near-ruination; how food was so scarce that it was difficult to know whether we or the animals would starve the first; and how it was the desperation of my hunger that had led me to raid his orchard.

The parson, whose name was Mr Trafford, now released me and, wiping his hand on the side of his shiny black jacket, as though what it had shortly been holding had somehow soiled it, he said: 'Well, boy, if you are so hungry, we had best see if Mrs Marley has something to feed you. I can well observe that you are a growing lad.' And at that he glanced down at the rend in my trousers and at what, willy-nilly, protruded through it. 'But cover yourself, boy, cover yourself, or you will be a scandal to others.' All that I could use to cover myself was my hand (and that was inadequate) until, in the parsonage, he found some trousers, evil-smelling and far too large, for me to put on in place of my own.

Mrs Marley, as crabbed as any apple in the orchard and Mrs only by courtesy, produced some victuals with an ill grace, setting them down on the study table, among the high-piled books, in a manner that suggested that she thought my proper place to be in the kitchen or even the byre. 'Eat, boy! Eat! Don't you like plum-cake?'

At first hesitantly and then gathering spirit, I began to gorge myself, while old Mr Trafford encouraged me with, 'That's a good boy! That's a good eating boy! Eat, boy, eat!'

When I was sated, I looked around me. I had never before in my life seen so many books, piled on the desk, on every table, in heaps on the floor. Nor had I ever before seen so many cats, sleeping among the books or on top of them, with saucers of cream, much of it rancid, and fragments of uncooked offal scattered here and there. One had jumped on Mr Trafford's knee and he was stroking it as he gazed at me while I was eating.

'Do you like books, boy?'

'I do not know any book but the Bible.'

'It is as well to begin with the best. After that, everything – like my own life – must inevitably be a declension. . . . Can you read, boy?'

'My foster-father, Mr Hill, reads to us from the Bible. I can read but little, sir.'

'That can be remedied. That *shall* be remedied.'

The eating of an apple once led to an expulsion from Paradise; but now the eating of an apple had led to my introduction to it. Whenever I could spare the time, I would come to my friend and would study with him how to write and read; how to add, subtract, multiply and divide; and finally how to master the Greek and Latin authors. He was a hard task-master and many was the time that I left the parsonage in tears, my posterior globes aflame and my heart resolved never to come back to it; but I was determined to make my eventual way in the world and, innocent that I then was, I did not understand that there was another, easier method of battering a road for myself to the top than through learning. The whole library was at my disposal, except for one bookcase, which was kept permanently locked. To this bookcase Mr Trafford kept the key on the same gold chain round his neck from which dangled a crucifix. He would often show me this key and say to me: 'When I have taught you everything in all these other books, then I shall give you this key so that you may also acquire knowledge of good and evil. The two are often interfused and the one mistaken for the other. After that, you will be ready to leave this little Paradise.' But alas, he died of a sudden catalepsy while fondling one of my knees as I sat reading Meleager beside him, and the key went, with all his other possessions, to his brother the earl. He had often told me that he would see that I was well set up in life (running his fingers through my hair or along my arm at the same time) but like many another, he no doubt thought himself to be immortal and made no testament in which he set out his wishes. I have neither regret nor bitterness on this score. If my father bequeathed to me the greatest of all possessions that a man can enjoy, my patron bequeathed to me the second greatest: knowledge.

At the time that I was a frequenter of Mr Trafford's parsonage, my foster-brother, a surly, cloddish man, and his shrewish wife would often make to me insinuating remarks about the old man, that I was then too innocent to grasp. Unlike many of his kind, however (as I shall later show) he was never in any way unmannerly to me, confining himself to an occasional caress, a stroking of the thigh, the knee or the buttock, an occasional kiss, not on the lips but on the forehead or the cheek, all of which I took for no more than a demonstration of avuncular affection.

Soon my grief at the loss of this dear and good, if curmudgeonly man, was compounded by the obvious decline of my foster-mother. Her ample form dwindled, her eyes lost their brightness and it became a labour for her even to prepare our simple meals. I did all that I was able to help her, drawing the water on her account, peeling the potatoes and sweeping the little cottage. Often when I was half-asleep at night, I would become aware of her slipping into my room like a phantom to plant a gentle kiss on my forehead. It is now my shame that I never then stirred, but pretended to sleep on, embarrassed by this show of a love that I nonetheless reciprocated.

On her deathbed she said to me: 'Danny, I have no fears for you. God has given you the wherewithal to achieve whatever you desire in life.' She had often told me that I had a good heart and I assumed then that it was to this that she was alluding. Perhaps, saintly woman that she was, it was indeed so; or perhaps she knew, wise woman that she also was, that there is something more potent than a good heart in attaining that heart's desire.

My foster-brother's wife now came daily to the house to look after my foster-father, often trailing her brood of lumpish, dirty and ill-mannered children behind her. She had no intention of looking after me and treated me as though she were a great lady and I a servant. Her animosity towards me may, in part at least, have been caused by an incident when I was some eleven or twelve years old and the two of us found ourselves alone in the house. Leaning over the table in a provocative manner, while I was deep in the study of a copy of Pliny lent to me by my patron, she suddenly cried out, 'Lawks!' and I saw that one of her breasts had flopped free of its ill-laced bodice and was now dangling out like the ear of a spaniel. She shook it before me as though it were some tempting prize, squinting at me lasciviously the while, until the evident alarm and repugnance on my face made her thrust it back into confinement with the observation that I had no business to stare in such an impudent manner when an untoward accident befell her through no fault of her own.

Weighed down with years and grief for his beloved wife, my foster-father soon followed her to the grave. My foster-brother and his monstrous family then moved into the house that for so many years I had regarded as my home and, though they did not actually expel me from it, they made it clear that my presence was far from welcome to them. I was given all the most menial chores about the farm and house, sweeping out the dung from the byres and emptying the night-soil from the privies. The children never ceased to torment me, the oldest of them, a cross-eyed boy of seven or eight, impudently pointing down and asking, 'What is that *thing* over there? Is it a bull's pizzle?'

One day, worn and sweat-stained from my work at the hoe and tired and tormented by this ceaseless goading and jibing, I wandered over the fields to where a rivulet made a bend under a tangle of verdurous branches. Here I found a pleasing shady recess, commodious to undress and leave

22

my clothes under, after which I plunged into the cooling waters. Little did I know that in the ancient summer-house on the opposite bank the daughter of the local squire, Lucy Atkins, had taken her work-basket in retreat from the midday sun. As she later told me the story, she was roused from the cane couch in which she had disposed herself by the sound of my splashing. Imagine her emotions when she peered through the window and discovered a naked youth floating on his back before her, in such a manner that she could not escape observing, try how she might, the black mossy tuft out of which appeared to emerge a round, softish, limber, white *something* of prodigious size! Maidenly modesty commanded her to turn her eyes away and continue with her embroidery of a chaircover for her great-aunt's birthday present; but the fire of nature, that had so long lain dormant in this sweet, innocent girl, began to break out and make her feel her sex for the first time. To observe the better, she leant even more heavily against the frame of the window which, the ancient wood being rotten, all at once collapsed before her, precipitating her out on the verandah of the summer-house in a state of fainting consternation. I heard her cry and swam hurriedly over to her; at which her cries, instead of abating, were redoubled. Through the half-open door I spied a shawl and, seizing this, I wrapped it round my loins. The maiden had now again fainted clean away at the rebuff to her modesty, lying all discomposed on the verandah with one leg revealed almost to the thigh. I knelt beside her where she had started to flutter like some poor wounded partridge, kissed her hand many times and begged her to forgive me, the tears in my eyes. By degrees she began to rally, with many a sigh and many a little sob. The fact that I was still stark-naked but for the inadequate protection of the shawl seemed now to have become less of an affront to her modesty, already so much wounded. With the utmost fear of offending anew, I again kissed both her hands and then, much daring, ventured to kiss her lips, which she neither declined nor resented. I then

23

carried her in my arms into the summer-house and placed her once again on the cane couch, in order that she might fully recover from the shock and terror that I had dealt to her.

Let it not be assumed that what followed was in any way unmannerly; we were both too youthful and too innocent to do more than marvel at each other, to exchange kisses, caresses and sighs and to vow eternal love. It is true that, on subsequent occasions when we met clandestinely in the summer-house, my fair captive asked me, with the utmost modesty, if she might view once again the instrument of her fainting-fit; and she even begged to touch it, doing so as though it were an eel; but seeing it growing sensibly before her gaze, she turned away with exclamations of terror. Her own sphere of Venus she refused to disclose to me, even though I was allowed the full liberty of her snow-white bosom, presenting on the vermilion summit of each pap the idea of a rose about to blow.

This idyll seemed likely never to end. My Lucy was at once the most artless and artful of companions; and though of a noble birth far above my bastardy, had no compunction in gathering a flower such as myself from a dung-hill. She would talk to me with all her natural charm and wit or listen to me, her tongue leaning negligently towards the lower range of her white teeth, whilst the natural ruby colour of her lips glowed with heightened life at my disquisitions on the wisdom of Plato or the exploits of Caesar. But unfortunately there was a serpent in our Paradise: one of my foster-brother's repugnant brood, the cross-eyed boy of whom I have already made mention, seeing me often to make my way towards the rivulet and curious of my business there, followed me by stealth, creeping from bush to bush. Observing my fair Lucy and me enter the summer-house together after I had washed myself in the waters, she meanwhile lying out on the verandah in a state of languid absorption in the spectacle of my manhood, he rushed off to inform first my foster-brother and then those at the Big House. The

Squire, convinced that I must have robbed his daughter of her most prized possession, threatened to have me horsewhipped if I stayed in the parish; and even a subsequent examination and the discovery that nothing irretrievable had been filched from her, failed to deflect his ire. Meanwhile my foster-brother and his shrewish wife, delighted to have yet further occasion to reproach me and humiliate me, never ceased to rail at me for the shame that I had brought down on their heads. It was then that I decided, all converse with my dearest Lucy now being denied to me, to set off for London, there to make my fortune. With much difficulty, I extracted from my foster-brother the small hoard of coins that, received from my mother, my dear foster-parents had kept in store for me; and so I took to the road, my heart heavy at the loss of my beloved and my luggage light.

2

Like Dick Whittington, I set off with a bundle tied to the
end of a stick, containing all my worldly goods; but unlike
him, I had no cat with me. It was not long however before
I had a bitch for travelling companion, for as I marched
down the highway, in my little flapped hat, kersey frock
and breeches and yearn stockings, whistling to myself, I
soon saw a wench, sitting on a stile and weeping bitterly.
She glanced up at me as I passed, as though inviting me to
speak to her and ask her her trouble; but my thoughts were
all of my beloved Lucy, even though this plump Niobe,
her blue eyes streaming not merely with tears but with an
inexpressible sweetness, was replete with attractions.

All on a sudden I became aware that she was now
trailing disconsolately behind me, shifting her bundle from
slender arm to arm and from time to time emitting yet
another heart-rending sob. At last I could not forbear, out
of pity, to ask her what had befallen her to cause her so
much woe. She at once regaled me with a story of a
father and mother, well-to-do farmers in country not
far distant from the village from which I myself had come,
who vouchsafed to bestow all their tenderness on a ne'er-
do-well son while treating her with the utmost barbarity;
of her breaking of a chamber-pot, the pride and idol of
both their hearts, and their threats to administer an
unmerciful beating; of her resolve to escape punishment
by leaving the house and making her way to London to
seek her fortune. 'Then we are two of a kind,' I told her,
'for I too am escaping from a barbarous treatment at
home and I too wish to seek my fortune. Let us keep

company together till we reach our journey's end.' What her designs were, I then knew not: the innocence of mine and my continuing fidelity to my beloved Lucy, I can solemnly protest.

As night drew on, inclement and raw, it became us to look out for some inn or shelter; to which perplexity another was added, and that was, what we should say for ourselves if we were questioned? After some puzzle, the wench started a proposal which I thought the finest that could be; and what was that? Why that we should pass for husband and wife. Of the consequences of this deception I never once dreamed. We came presently, after having agreed on this notable expedient, to one of those paltry hedge-accommodations for foot passengers, at the door of which stood an old crazy beldame, stinking of gin and pot-grease, who seeing us trudge by, invited us to lodge there. Glad of any cover, however poor, we went in and, taking all upon me, I called for what the house could afford, and we supped together as man and wife; which considering our ages could not have passed on anyone but such as anything in the whole world could pass on. But when bed-time came on I had not the courage to contradict my first account of ourselves and my companion seemed equally reluctant. While we were in this quandary, our landlady, the candle in her hand as she chewed on a wad of tobacco with her toothless gums, bade us make haste, saying that she still had much to do, and lighted us to our squalid apartment through a long yard. Thus we suffered ourselves to be conducted without saying a word in opposition; and there in a wretched room, containing nought but a sagging cot, we were left to pass the night together, the landlady giving us a villainous wink out of her rheumy eye as she wished us good repose.

Still saying no word to each other, we began to undress after I had blown out the candle. My teeth all a-chatter, I pulled one of the threadbare coverlets off the bed, in preparation to sleep as best I might on a floor spread with dirty straw; but the wench, already nestled within the bed, told me in a faint voice that I should catch my death of cold, the door fitting so ill and the pane of the window being broken and inadequately stuffed with rags. 'Let us share the bed,' she urged. 'With such a decent gentleman as yourself I am sure that no maid can come to harm.' At that, still somewhat reluctant but overborne by her pleading, I crept under the clothes. But I could not sleep, not so much because of the coldness as by the novelty of my position, so near to this beauteous wench. In all honesty, I had not the least thought of harm; but after a while she murmured 'Ah, but it is cold!' and moved over towards me as though to take heat as from a fire. Oh! how powerful are the instincts of nature! how little is there wanting to set them in action! The warmth that I felt from joining our breasts kindled another and, before I was fully cognizant with what was happening, we were kissing each other. All at once the little vixen slipped her hand down from my breast, the nascent hairs of which she had been playfully tugging, to the part of me where the sense of feeling is so exquisitely critical and at once exclaimed: 'Oh no, sir! For pity, sir! Have mercy on a virgin! Such an instrument as that would split me from crown to toe!' Yet she continued to fondle me, relishing the proud distinction between her sex and mine, at the same time drawing my own hands to her own seat of pleasure. To cut a long story short, in no time at all she had arranged the pillows under her abundant curls, her legs were around my thighs and we were swiving merrily; yet all the time she continued to cry out, so loud that I was affeared that the other lodgers would hear us, 'Oh, no, sir! Have pity, sir! I cannot support it!' When she repeated this 'I cannot support it!' in a heartrending manner several times over, I felt obliged to withdraw; but at that she at once grappled closer to me, changing her tune to, 'I can *hardly* support it!' There was much more about her being a virgin and my despoiling her, but in view of the size of my weapon and the ease with which I was able to sheath it in her scabbard, I now disbelieve her protestations; but at that time I was too innocent of the ways of women to suspect her for a lying jade.

After I had been no less than four times to the selfsame well, I fell off into a deep sleep, as much from the exertions of the bed as of the road. Though the maid bemoaned once again the cruel necessity that obliged her sex to gather the first honey of love off lacerating thorns, I did not then have the wit to relight the candle and see if indeed her passage through the thorns or the passage of my thorn through her had left any bleeding testimony. When I awoke, it was to find that my pride of nature had already woken before me, so that I had to shift my position to achieve a greater comfort. Then I opened my eyes and saw that the jade had woken even earlier still and that she and her bundle had both disappeared. I leapt from the bed and began to pull on my clothes, until it was all at once borne in on me, with the shock of a thunderclap, that the leather pouch in which I had been carrying my small hoard of coins, fastened about my waist, had vanished with her. In a frenzy, I hunted high and low, even hurling the wretched mattress, gaping straw at every hole, on to the floor and overturning the chamber-pot. Though naturally honest and god-fearing from the instruction received both from my beloved parents and from the parson, I could see nothing for it but to make my escape without payment of my dues; and to this end I pushed open the broken window with the intention to climb out of it. But on the other side, invisible because of the rags that took the place of panes, I was confronted with the spectacle of our landlady, mucky skirts hitched up over purple-veined thighs, seated at her matutinal duty in the jakes. She let out a scream and I let out an oath; she jumped up and I jumped down. Not long after that, she entered the hovel in which I was cowering and, arms akimbo while she continued to chew on a wad of tobacco, demanded of me why I should spy on an innocent woman in such a blackguardly fashion. Concluding that I should lose nothing by frankness, I told her the whole story of the lying wench and her theft from me; at which she roared at me that she was not such a one to be cheated by two vagrants, that she would have the beadle on me and that in no time at all I should be expiating the sins of myself and my companion in the stocks. I begged her to forbear and have mercy on me and soon saw that, with many a downward glance to my kersey breeches, she was on the way to relenting.

'Very well,' she said at last, spitting out the wad of tobacco far farther than many a man would be able to do. 'If I do you a service, then you must needs do me one.'

I assented to the logic of this proposition, assuming that she would set me some duty such as cleaning out the malodorous jakes in which I had suprised her, fetching water or hewing wood. But she thumped down on the cot, with such a force that I thought that it were nigh to break, and beckoned me towards her. I had no notion of what was in her mind, having never before heard of such a custom, and could not forbear to cry out, 'Please, madam! Madam, no!' But what use were it for someone like myself, alone and penniless, to make any further protestation or resistance? As she chewed on something more substantial than her wad of tobacco with her toothless gums, showing a skill infinitely superior to her looks, I bethought me of my former home, of my happy hours in the parsonage and, above all, of my darlingest Lucy.

Once finished, the villainous beldame wiped her moustache and told me, 'Now we are quits. Last night you consumed my substance and this morning I have consumed yours.' But at a loss how I should fare on the road with not a penny in my pocket, I was emboldened to ask if she could not perhaps spare me a coin or two. 'A service requires a service,' she said, rising now from the cot; and once again I was obliged to assent to the logic of this proposition, saying, 'Anything you wish, ma'am.' She then bid me to await her, threatening that if I were to make any manner of move to escape she would at once have first the dogs and then the beadle on me, and went from the chamber, well satisfied with her work. You may guess in what a state of anxiety I awaited her return and what were my feelings of repulsion and horror when she returned with another beldame, even uglier, muckier and grosser, if that were possible, than her own bedraggled self. Cackling in high glee, the newcomer thumps down on the cot, while the other stands over us, arms akimbo, and once again I needs must think of my former home, of my happy hours in the parsonage and, above all, of my darlingest Lucy, in order to distract myself.

Having done with me, the second witch wiped her moustache in the same manner as the first and then, having risen to her feet, had a brief whispered converse with her infernal sister. She then searched among her rags and tatters and found two or three paltry coins with which to reward me. Seeing me gaze down at these in my palm with visible disappointment, she shrilled: 'Be satisfied with such generosity! It is the stronger that usually must pay recompense to the fairer sex!'

'But, madam,' I stammered, my legs failing me both from my recent exercise and from despair for my lot, 'how shall I support myself all the way to London town on such a fee as this?'

The first beldame then commanded me to wait, again threatened to have the dogs and the beadle on me if I were to make an attempt to effect an escape and she and her sister then left the chamber. Again you may guess in what a state of anxiety I awaited their return and what were my feelings of repulsion and horror when they returned to usher in before them a man, bearded and blood-shot as to the eyes, of such antiquity that he might have been old Father Time himself. At this I doubted whether any thoughts of my former home, of my happy hours in the parsonage and even of my darlingest Lucy would avail to distract me and I cried out that I had had enough and must resume my journey forthwith. There were cries of first disappointment and then anger from the three, the two harpies plucking at the sleeves of my kersey frock as though to tear it, while their brother frenziedly plucked at me somewhere else. But I tore myself away from them and, my little bundle dangling from my stick, the dogs yapping and snarling at my heels and the three calling after me, now to curse and now to cajole, I set my face towards London and the fortune that I proposed to make there.

Weary and travel-stained, my belly as empty as my pockets, I at last reached the metropolis to find its streets paved, not with gold, but with cobbles exceedingly harsh to my already sore feet. No less harsh were the people who, on my asking them for work or even directions, barely gave me a civil answer. Eventually, as I was trudging through the vicinity of Shepherd Market, whistling dolefully to myself to keep my spirits up while I began to wish that I had not exchanged the barbarous treatment that I had lately received in the village for this total negligence of me here, I espied a woman of an extraordinary beauty seated at her embroidery frame in the window of a house of noble proportions. Though it seemed to me that here was obviously a lady of the highest quality, hung about as she was with jewellery and her neck and shoulders of a milk-white perfection, I could not but halt and stare at this vision; at which to my amaze, she lowers her needle and beckons me over. Guessing that she must intend some reprimand for my impudent staring, I stammered out, 'Pray forgive me, my lady. I know that it is unmannerly for me to gaze thus through your window but for a moment I thought that you must be a dream bred out of my weariness and lack of any food.'

At this she laughed most merrily, throwing back her head in such a manner that beneath the flimsy gauze thrown across her bosom, I could glimpse her rosy paps, like the shy muzzles of two leverets. 'The customer may view the goods in a shop without being beholden to purchase,' she told me; to which I retorted, not fully understanding her drift, 'Alas, my lady, I am in no way to make any purchase, even of a loaf of bread.'

She had been eyeing me up and down during this speech,

as though in doubt how to make up her mind; then she said, 'Your pockets may be empty but your breeches seem to be uncommonly full.'

I was indeed becoming sensible, even as I glanced again at those two rosy paps behind their veil of gauze, that my breeches were growing uncomfortably confining. 'If you wish to enter, then perhaps I can satisfy your appetite, in part at least, with no charge.'

At my assenting eagerly to this proposition, deeming my straits to be such that they did not admit of pride, she despatched her Abigail, a mulatto of more than normal size teetering on heels of such a height that you would have thought them to be stilts, to open up the door to me. Once within, my mind, used to the rural simplicities of my foster-parents' cottage and the sober disorder of the parsonage, could not but be dazzled by such a profusion of pink and purple damask and brocade, gilt chairs and tables and pretty knick-knacks. My lady rustled towards me and, as she did so, my empty belly set up a protest at its long fast, thus causing me to blush hotly and her to laugh loudly. 'I see,' she said, 'that we must first fill one vessel before we fill the other. Show all despatch, Beulah –' she had now turned to the mulatto serving-wench – 'and bring this poor wayfarer some viands before Mr Gurnsey returns.' With a hoity-toity toss of her head, this Beulah made off on her high shoes but, catching the pointed heel of one on a Turkey carpet, she stumbled forward and was only saved by my seizing her before she fell to the ground. 'Enough of such tricks!' said her mistress with ill humour, though the fall seemed the most natural thing in the world to me. While Beulah was in the nether regions, the lady then explained to me that Mr Gurnsey was her 'ruffian', a word the precise connotation of which was then not known to me and which I assumed to be fashionable parlance for a husband.

'Pray set to!' she commanded, as soon as the viands had been set down before me, Beulah bending so low that I could not forbear to take a hurried glance down her happy

33

valley. 'We have little time to spare, for Mr Gurnsey, who is gone about a debt on my behalf, will return before long.' I needed no further bidding and at once began to gobble cold chicken, pasties and sweetmeats all pell-mell between copious gulps of the finest Rhenish wine. The lady gazed at me in obvious amazement and delight at so prodigious an appetite, having already despatched the reluctant Beulah. It was as I was biting into a lemon comfit that she jumped up with an exclamation of 'Enough, sir! Enough! To work!' threw herself down on to a couch and raised petticoats and shift to display not merely the finest turned legs and thighs that could be imagined but also a full view of that delicious cleft of flesh in which the pleasing hair-grown mount parted and presented a most inviting entrance between two close-hedges, delicately soft and pouting. At this unexpected spectacle, I suffered an instant petrifaction, my vital forces being in such high plight that I must perforce remove my breeches for fear of splitting them and having no other pair. Let me not linger on the turtle-billing, kisses and poignant, painless love-bites; on the wreathing and intertwistings of limbs together; on the violence with which I finally gave her the spurs and her own concert of springy heaves, like a mare in full canter; and her final, 'Oh, Sir! . . . Good Sir! . . . Pray do not spare me! ah! ah! ah!' as we cleared the final hurdle.

A moment later Beulah ran into the room, crying, 'God save us, madam, Mr Gurnsey has but even now ridden up to the house, with a gentleman whom I take to be a customer!' The lady jumped up from her languorous swoon, reassembling her dress and meantimes telling me, in the most urgent tones, to despatch and on no account whatsoever to reveal what had passed between us, for, as she put it to my then bewilderment, 'If any chance comer may pick up a diamond in the dust, then no one who follows will pay the due price for it.' While I was still buttoning my breeches, the balsamic efflux not yet dry, she gave me a push, crying, 'Begone, sir! Begone! And remember – no word to any soul!'

Beulah clattered down the back-stair and I hurried after her, smoothing my dishevelled locks with my hands, the laces of my shoes untied and one hose gathered about my ankle. We emerged into a yard at the rear of the house when, all on a sudden, the mulatto wench spins round and throws her arms round me, gluing her lips to mine as she murmurs, 'Ah, Moses, dearest Moses!' Since Moses was not my name, I was as much surprised by this form of address as by conduct that might well be viewed from any adjacent window. But then I glimpsed the man, with the battered face and stalwart physique of a prize-fighter, who was entering the gate, and saw her ruse.

'What is this?' he bellowed.

'Oh, sir! I'm sure I'm sorry, sir! But my cousin has late arrived from the Indies and has called to see me!'

'Send him about his business, and prepare the bed-chamber with clean linen and bring some sherry wine. Your mistress is entertaining!'

'Yes, sir! Indeed, sir! I beg your pardon, sir!' At that the girl gave me a thrust out of the gate and I took to my heels, wondering if my Italian complexion were really so dusky as to have me mistaken for a mulatto's cousin.

Sated in all my appetites, I walked lethargically down the street, eventually to find my way to Park Lane, where an old blind woman was begging in the dust at a corner. As I passed, I heard her exclaim: 'Lawks! Such a size would not seem possible!'

Since there was no one else at hand, I presumed that it was of me that she was speaking and, turning, said: 'What the eye does not see, the heart should not rejoice over!'

At this sally, the old harridan laughed and said: 'How else is a poor, abandoned woman like myself, her husband lost in the wars and her health lost in the stews, to earn her daily bread except by a deception? Do not be hard on me, kind sir, but on a world so insensible to any misfortune other than that which obtrudes on it as insistently as that good fortune of yours.'

Again she shook her bowl, coaxing me: 'Kind sir, I see that you have a gentle face! As you start out on your road to triumph, have pity on one who has come to the end of her road to ruin!' I did indeed have pity on her, fancying that I saw in her saddle-nose, rheumy eyes and twisted limbs the buxom country-girl that once she had been; but I needs must explain my situation to her, without either prospects or pence. At that the good soul drew a penny out of her bowl with two grimy fingers and bade me to take it to help me on my way.

'No, no, that I cannot do,' I retorted, 'but at least tell me where I may find some honest work to earn me a bed and a crust.'

'All work is honest,' she replied, 'unless it be thieving or cheating,' and she then gave me directions to an intelligence office, not far off in Piccadilly, where I might get information of a place such as a country boy like myself, well-spoken and not unlettered, might be fitted for. Promising that, if all should go well with me, I should some day return to recompense her for her kindness, I went on my way; but such is the shortness of human memory and the shallowness of human gratitude that the old crone passed entirely from my mind until I set down the above account.

The intelligence office was kept by an elderly woman, dressed all in black bombazine with an eyeglass on a pinchbeck chain round her neck, who sat at the receipt of custom, her posture rigidly correct, with a book before her in great form and order and several scrolls, ready made out, of directions of places. I made up to this important person, conscious of my dust-stained and well-worn shoes and dirty clothes, without lifting up my eyes to observe any of the people who were attending there on the same errand as myself and, bowing deeply, just made a shift to stammer out my need.

Madam, having heard me out with all the gravity of brow of a petty minister of State listening to some underling, then made me no answer but to ask of me a pre-

36

liminary shilling, with which I was, of course, unable to furnish her. She then told me that, without the payment of the preliminary shilling, there was nothing she could do for me and she would be obliged if I would retire so that she might despatch some other customers. At this an elderly dame, of the stature of a grenadier, her face heavily painted and her person extravagantly bedizened, dressed in a purple velvet mantle with a bonnet of the same hue, rose from her seat in the corner and made a stately progress over to us. While I had been talking to the proprietress of the establishment, I had indeed been conscious of this beldame's staring at me from head to foot or, rather, from waist to knee, without the least regard to propriety or good manners. Now she said, in a voice so deep that it seemed as though it were emerging from Acheron: 'Sweetheart, do you want a place?'

The familiarity of the address surprised me no less than the profundity of its tone. But deeming that beggars could not be choosers, I assented, 'Yes, and please you, my lady,' at the same time executing a deep bow towards her.

Upon this she acquainted me that she was come to the office to look out for someone just such as myself, a country boy of good looks and obvious substance, to serve in her shop; that her custom was only of the highest quality; that London was a very wicked place, a veritable Sodom and Gomorrah; and that she hoped that I would be tractable and obedient to all her instructions and demands and keep myself out of any such bad company as might bring disgrace on her and her highly respectable business. While she was apprising me of all this, I could not help but notice how she and the good woman in black bombazine (the latter now holding her eye-glass raised as she quizzed me impertinently) kept exchanging shrewd looks, smirks and even winks; but I assumed, in my innocence, that these were merely marks of their pleasure at having reached so speedy an accommodation.

The business being concluded, my mistress, who informed me that her name was Mrs Swellington summoned, a coach and bade the coachman drive me to a shop close by St Paul's Churchyard, where she proceed to buy me a quantity of clothes of an elegance such as I had never possessed before, all regardless of expense. As she looked me over in now a nankeen jacket and now a lace cravat, she explained the whiles that in an establishment as select as hers all the servants must be accoutred in the utmost finery. When I commented on the price of her purchases, she commanded me to think nothing of it and led me on to a cobbler's, where she found some shoes ordered by a gentleman and never claimed or paid for, that exactly fitted my foot and then bade the cobbler make three other pairs to the same last. I could only conclude that, by the greatest good fortune, I had fallen into the hands of the kindest of mistresses; and this was born out by her repeated use of 'sweetheart', 'dear boy', 'dear child' etc. to me and the affectionate manner in which she patted my knee or tweaked my cheek.

As we were travelling to her house in ——— Street she complained of the stuffiness in the carriage, wiped her brow on her sleeve with an inelegance hardly befitting a lady of her rank, sighed, kicked off a shoe, grunted and loosened her lacing. I was surprised to observe how hirsute was the flesh thus revealed of her bosom but knew from experience how in old age the paths that separate the two sexes from each other begin to converge again, as once they did in infancy. Gathering my courage, I asked what exactly would be the duties required of me in my new position. 'Well, sweetheart,' she began and then seemed at a loss how to continue. But eventually she told me, now mopping at that sweating bosom with a kerchief inserted with one hand into her bodice, that her business was some species of joinery; that I need have no fears on the ground of my lack of experience of the trade, since it was one easily mastered by someone possessed of all my natural attributes; that borers, screws, shanks, reamers, perforators, piercers, stop-cocks, rammers, rods, pistons, indeed every species of tool, vent and vice would become familiar to me in no time at all; that I should learn how to appreciate a well-turned leg, a firm-set bottom or a shapely breast-rail; that the services of her work-shop were available only to the very best kind of customer, people of substance and quality, who could not come there except on recommendation; and that in consequence both personal cleanliness and neatness and total discretion were essential. She concluded: 'But it is rarely that I am mistaken when I engage any persons for my staff. I have an eye for hidden potentialities and, with the rudiments of my training, there is no reason why you should not become a master in your field.' Such was still my innocence that I imagined that it was the intention of Mrs Swellington to make of me another Mr Chippendale or Mr Sheraton.

You may be sure that my opinion of my good fortune was not lessened by our arrival at a handsome house, set back in its garden and overshaded by medlar and mulberry trees, and our entry into a back parlour in which stood two pier-glasses and a buffet. My new mistress called out, 'Harriet! Harriet! Drat the girl! What has become of her? Harriet!' fanning herself the while with her sweat-soaked handkerchief. 'This heat!' The autumnal weather did not seem to me hot but no doubt with so much velvet and damask on her back and so much paint on her face, not to mention the peruke that towered, like some miniature St Paul's, over her crimson, beaky countenance, she might well feel the need for coolness. Eventually a trim little figure slipped into the room, as small and sober as her mistress was large and extravagant, dropped a curtsey and apologized for her absence, saying that she had just been drawing the cream from the milkman. 'Fie on you, girl!' her mistress upbraided her. 'I have a prodigious thirst and require a tankard of ale.' She then pointed at me and said: 'And here, Harriet, I have just hired this young gentleman, Mr Danny Hill, who is come to learn the business.'

'Mr Danny Hill! Can he be any relative of that hoity-toity hussy Fanny Hill?' the maidservant asked.

'I know not and care not,' her mistress answered before I could say that my foster-parents had indeed been the parents of a daughter called Fanny Hill; and from my mistress's tone I then surmised that it would be better for me to continue to hold my peace. She went on: 'I charge you to use him with as much respect as you would myself. I have taken a prodigious liking to him and I do not know what I shall not do for him.' The maidservant darted me a demure look from under lustrous lashes, from which it was evident to me that she too had taken a prodigious liking even at so brief an acquaintance. 'Until that d——d journeyman has completed his hanging of the best bed-room, he will be obliged to sleep along with you. But he is, as you can see, a young man not merely of parts but of the strictest propriety and I can vouch that no harm will overtake you. You may show him your chamber and guide him how to dispose his impedimenta. But be sure that you lay no hand on them!' With this last strict injunction, we left her presence.

As we mounted the handsome staircase, the girl prattling encomiums on her good mistress! her sweet mistress! and how happy I was to light upon her! that I could not have bespoke a better! and other such like gross stuff that would itself have started suspicions in any but such an unpractised simpleton as myself, I wondered that there was no sign of any workshop or of any other workers. Eventually, I questioned the girl on this point, to which she replied, with some obfuscation, that most of the workers came in by the hour and that of the three who were regular and resident, one was lying sick and the remaining pair were both out on errands. But all those who were concerned with Mrs Swellington were such proper, handsome gentleman, as I should shortly learn for myself. At this she showed me into a neat room, where was a single large bed and, to my surprise, a pair of breeches and a shirt in addition to a profusion of female clothing. Not wishing to embarrass the girl by asking the provenance of shirt and breeches, I feigned not to have observed them even though they lay across the bed. 'I am instructed not to lay hands on your impedimenta,' the girl simpered at me, 'and I durst not disobey my mistress, dearly though I should wish to do so. I shall therefore quit you, leaving you to make your own way down to the parlour when you are ready. We shall become better acquainted, I hope, very shortly.' At that she gazed at me for a long time under her lustrous lashes and then took her leave.

Having set out my new possessions, I eventually returned to the parlour, where to my astonishment I found my mistress lying full length on the couch, her shoes now kicked off, her bodice open to the waist to reveal a bosom even more hairy than I had at first suspected and most wondrous of all, her wig tilted so far askew that I could see that there were but scant hairs, and those short cropped, on her head. In her hand she was holding a tankard of prodigious size, to contain at least a quart, from which she was quaffing the ale, with all the gusto of a sailor just back in port or a ploughman just returned from the fields. Only then did I realize (the reader can guess with what consternation horror and disgust) that this beldame was, in very truth, of the same sex as myself.

Observing my expression, Mr Swellington (for I can no longer accord him the title of Mrs, however much he may have wished to appropriate it) raised the tankard to me, saying: 'My dear Danny, I drink to your future prosperity and the health on which that prosperity will depend!' He drained the tankard at a single gulp, eructated most inelegantly and then went on: 'Pray do not be so astonished. Most of what we are is what we dress ourselves as being: the judge no different from the criminal but for his robes and wig; the bishop from the sinner but for his lawn sleeves and pectoral cross; the squire from the labourer but for his well-cut jacket and silken hose; the grand lady from the trull but for her patches and panniers. You may perhaps deem that when I go abroad in my finery as Mrs Swellington, it is a confidence trick that I play on the public at large; but to win confidence it is

necessary to have confidence and to make others believe
it is necessary oneself to believe. Despite all the evidence
of these muscular arms and legs of mine –' thereat he
extended one leg towards me, hitching his skirts yet
higher – 'of the hair that grows on my chin and indeed
elsewhere in such profusion and, above all, of that one
small difference that is all the difference in the world, I
believe and therefore I am – *credo ergo sum*. If we may
accept that an ageing harridan like Mrs Siddons is Juliet
or that a portly coxcomb like Mr Garrick is Hamlet, then
by the same token and the same persuader's art, may we
not accept that your master is a mistress? Cease all this
gawping and gasping and Harriet shall bring you a
tankard of ale. Where is the wench?' I declined this offer,
at that time being unused to the imbibing of spirituous
liquors, but Mr Swellington would have none of my demur,
exclaiming that since I was so palpably a man, I must
drink like a man. I refrained from asking why, if he were
so eager to pass for a woman, it was as a man, indeed as
two men, that he also drank.

Dinner being set on the table in another room, we were
joined thither by the two other regular workmen of the
establishment, Harriet having already taken to the third,
sick in his chamber, a bowl of broth and a coddled egg.
One of the two who were now my fellows was a villainous-
looking youth of oxlike frame, his shoulders almost as
wide as he was tall and his legs like twin oak-trunks. He
was dressed in the height of fashion and was at pains to
speak lispingly in the manner of some beau at the Court;
but many was the time when, in his excitement, he would
come out with some gruff and guttural syllable that
betrayed his lowly origins. His name was Samuel and he
seemed a good enough soul despite his frightsome appearance. There was an abundance of rings on his fingers,
flashing fire, and from time to time he would raise a
scented kerchief of the finest lawn to his nostrils with a
cry of, 'Lud!' or, 'Law!'.

The other was an Italian gentleman, Guido, as thin and

wriggling as any worm, whom I surmised to have seen not much less than fifty summers despite his boyish (or should I say girlish?) manner of movement and parlance. His voice was as disagreeably high-pitched as a chalk on a slate, for a reason that was only clear to me many days subsequently, when I learned from Harriet, an enthusiastic prattler, that he had once been one of those male nightingales so favoured in the opera, a brutal robbery having abstracted from his purse what may be accounted two of man's most valuable possessions; that for many years he had enjoyed the highest favour both in his native Milan and in all the cities of the civilized world; but that he had contracted some noxious disease from using his voice-box for some purpose other than that for which the Good Lord had intended it (in short, imbibing rather than giving forth honey) and had so lost its use. He had been pelted in Parma, booed in Bordeaux, hissed throughout the length of breadth of Hispania and all but lapidated in London; at last quitting the stage of his former triumphs and now of his shame, to serve Mr Swellington's clients with the same degree, but a different kind, of artistry as that with which he had once entertained the crowned heads of Europe. He was mighty civil to me, even, to my secret displeasure, popping the choicest morsels of food into my mouth with his long fingers, for all the world as if I were some lap-dog whom he must feed. To my surprise Harriet, though the serving-wench, joined us at the table. In the kitchen there were two other servants, an ancient beldame, crook-backed and cross-eyed but a cunning cook, and her grandson, a boy of some fourteen or fifteen years, who with his enormous head, as of a tadpole, and bulging eyes might well have earned money in a raree show.

Mr Swellington, who had first replaced both wig and shoes and tidied his disordered dress, presided at the table with all the dignity and nicety of a well-born lady at the family board. From time to time he would instruct me in manners, for I was unused to such a plethora of dishes and such a profusion of knives and forks and spoons. To Samuel he was far sharper than to me, instructing him, for example, that whereas in bed a man might cram both fork and mouth and no blame attached, at the board it was impolite to do so; that there are occasions when to go down was not merely permissible but even pleasurable but that to go down on food, rather than to raise it up to one's lips, was the sign of indifferent breeding; that to swill out every orifice was a precaution much to be recommended, but that it was unmannerly to do so with the wine or water in company. Samuel took all such correction in excellent part, being obviously eager to learn from his master-mistress how to become the fashionable gentleman as speedily as possible.

In contrast Guido needed no such instruction, being so nice, with the delicacy of his extended little finger, his dabbing at his lips with his napkin between every morsel taken, his nibbling as of a rabbit and his sipping as of a cat, that it was easy to see that he had for many long years been used to the best kind of company. As I ate and drank, most of the conversation being chiefly kept up by Mr Swellington and the serving-wench, in expressions often so outlandish to me that I could not understand their drift, I grew more and more pleased with the view that opened to me of an easy service under these people. Mr Swellington might indeed be eccentric, Harriet pert, Samuel bone-headed and Guido lacking in manly attraction; but it seemed to me that all were worthy souls, whose friendship I should come to value.

The repast over, Mr Swellington beckoned Samuel to come over to him and there followed a whispered conversation that, strain as I might, I could hear only in snatches. There was some mention of my Lady This or That; of a house in Curzon Street; of a certain sum of guineas, all this followed by insistent admonitions to come home as soon as his task was finished. I understood from all this that there must be some joinery of urgency to which, at this late hour, the fellow was being despatched.

44

Finally there were some injunctions about clothes, again hardly audible to me. After all this Samuel left us and hurried upstairs; at which Guido seated himself at the spinet and began to strum an air and Mr Swellington and Harriet settled themselves to a game of écarté, leaving me to peruse the daily news-sheet. Mr Swellington assured me that their evenings were not usually so dull, since the house attracted company almost nightly; but that there was some rout in progress at my Lady So-and-So's and, that all the quality must needs be present there. By and by Samuel returned, but so changed that I hardly recognized him, dressed as he was in a sailor's bell-bottomed trews and other matching gear, his brawny arms bare to display such a tattooing of mermaids and hearts and union jacks as I had never seen before in so riotous a profusion. But Mr Swellington, having quizzed him up and down like any Admiral inspecting a tar on parade, at once told him to remove the rings that still flashed their fires from his stubby fingers. Samuel showed a great reluctance to obey this order; and when he was at last persuaded, vast was the difficulty in wrenching off one after the other; but Mr Swellington was like adamant, reminding him that My Lady This would feel defrauded if she did not receive exactly what she had bargained for. Finally, the rings were all removed and placed for safe keeping in a bureau in one corner, Mr Swellington slipping the key to the drawer containing them into his bosom which, cunningly padded and compressed, gave all the semblance of a valley, albeit not a very happy or salubrious one. 'Lady This is most insistent that all trade that enters her mansion should be rough,' he explained to me when Samuel had quit the room. 'Many is the time that a whiff of perfume or a foot or armpit too carefully washed has reduced her to a state of fury. No man may drop his breeches to her unless he also drops his aitches.' I was bewildered by all this, wondering why her Ladyship should so concern herself with the humble joiner sent on some such errand as easing her casement or realigning her manteltree.

Guido now began to sing to his strumming, if indeed such a caterwauling, as of a tom submitting to even such an indignity as that to which the poor wretch had been subjected, can be dignified by such a term. Having no Italian, I could not even derive enjoyment from the words; and fearing that to block my ears would be an affront both to politeness and to his feelings, I made an excuse that I must needs slip out to the privy and left the room. Below stairs, I found the hydrocephalic tot scouring the pots while his grand-dam, seated, legs spread wide, on a rush-bottomed chair, was industriously sewing at some small linen bags. Having greeted her and made myself known, I enquired whether she made these bags for the sale of lavender to eke out her wages; to which she replied, leaving me little the wiser, that such commodity that they contained was sold by her mistress (she did not say master) not by herself. 'But though this is the finest Bogside linen,' she went on, 'bought I know not at what cost, many is the time that the horse, being so mettlesome, breaks down the stable door.' I could not get her drift and therefore enquired of her for the name of her grandson. She then informed me that he was Tommy; that, because of the unhappy misshapement of his body, she had feared that a life of denial and sadness must lie before him; but that the Lord had decreed in His goodness that there should always be someone for everyone and that a certain gentleman, an attorney and a scholar to boot, had taken compassion on the poor lad and doted on him marvellously. Previously this same kind gentleman had been the patron of a boy whose right leg had been crushed by a fall of coal in the mines; but the same boy had also soon contracted a consumption from his previous unsalubrious employment below the earth and the gentleman had rightly cast him off for fear of the contagion. 'Tommy is a healthy sprig,' she concluded, 'as you may see for your own eyes and the good gentleman will have no cause to cast him off in similar manner. He is such a saintly gentleman, whose only care is for the halt, the maimed and the blind.'

46

When Harriet eventually lighted me up to bed, I could not but think of the night that I had passed in that villainous lodging-place and of the parlous way in which my road-companion had used me; but in remembering the loss of my money with sadness, I also remembered the loss of another possession with pleasure. Would Harriet prove equally complaisant? I asked of myself as I observed her two posterior globes moving ahead of me, in most diverting fashion, up the staircase. Once in the chamber, she blew out the candle as it had been blown out on that previous occasion, and, become all at once strangely silent, began to divest herself whilst I did likewise. I strained my eyes to make out something of her form but the night was a dark one and all I could observe was the occasional glimmer of those twin moons at her rear.

I was already slipped between the bed-covers when, with a light sigh, she slipped in beside me. For a while we lay thus, breathing quietly beside each other, I fearful to make the smallest move lest she summon Mr Swellington and cause a scandal in the house and she, as I supposed, already in the arms of Morpheus and with no intention of entering mine. Then, of a sudden, with another sigh, she turned to me and our two bodies met against each other. I had supposed her to be in the sixteenth or seventeenth year but from the absence of hillocks such as I had explored with the jade that had so wantonly cheated me and robbed me, I now resolved that she must be even younger. 'Sweetheart,' she murmured. 'My mopsey, jewel, honey, precious, angel, fondling.' At that her hands became extremely free and wandered over my whole body with touches, squeezes, pressures that set me all afire. But each time that I myself attempted the main spot, she would squirm away from me, compressing her narrow thighs together and distracting me with repeated kisses and cries such as, 'OH! Here is meat fit for a queen! . . . Would that you could make a woman of me! . . . What a charming creature you are!' and things of a similar nature. At last, in a tempest of passion provoked by her

47

skill, I insisted on steering my ship to haven; when, to my amazement and consternation, I discovered that instead of finding anchorage in an inlet, I was battering against a promontory.

'What may be this?' I cried, to which the wench replied, 'What do you think that it may be?', at the same time deftly flinging her legs about my waist. For a second I hesitated; then, being apprehensive of the raging waves that threatened to spill the cargo of my barque, methought, 'Heigho! Any port in a storm!' and I followed where my cunning pilot guided me. It was easy to see that I was not first to berth there, despite her frantic cries of, 'Attend! Attend! Some goose-grease, my mopsey!' to which I paid no heed. Our play done, I fell asleep, through pure weariness from the violence of the emotions I had been led into; but ere ever the night was over nature recompensed me for this simulacrum of true pleasure with one of those dreams, itself a simulacrum but a far more luscious one and scarce inferior to the waking action that it represented, of my beloved, lost Lucy and myself in each other's arms.

In the morning I awoke about ten, my head and heart equally heavy after what had befallen. The sun, glimpsed through the curtains, was shining brightly and I feared that I must be late for my work and that Mr Swellington would discharge me for negligence. To my great amazement, the cunning partner of my previous night's enjoyment was still slumbering beside me, his little upturned nose emitting an unattractive snorting and snuffling as of a pig in search of mast. I shook him awake with some rudeness and said: 'We are late. We must be about our duties.' He opened his eyes, blinking them as though to expel what the sandman had scattered there and then asked me, in a petulant tone, what was troubling me. 'My work,' I replied. 'It is the first day of my work and I needs must show Mr Swellington my diligence and punctuality.'

To this he retorted, greatly surprising me: '*Mrs

Swellington –' he emphasized the Mrs, in correction of me – 'Mrs Swellington, our mistress, has no need of our services until long after noon. The quality do not call until then, having danced, drunk or dallied the whole night away, and our mistress herself certainly will not be risen. But let us observe how far you yourself are risen,' he went on, making an impudent attempt beneath the bedclothes, which I indignantly repulsed.

'What ails you?' he cried out then. 'So hot in the night and so cold in the day! This is paradoxical!'

'For what happened last night I am both ashamed and sorry. A clasp leads to a kiss; a kiss to a caress; a caress to a cuddle. After that, what full-blooded man can reserve himself from coddling and cockering? But frankness, no less than decency, bids me tell you that you have played a scurvy trick on me.'

At that the creature snickered and, glancing up at me from under those wondrously lustrous eyelashes, chid me, 'There are none so easy to trick but those who wish to be so. But each man can but follow his own natural bent, however unnatural it may be. I do not hold your conduct against you and I doubt if Mrs Swellington will do so, since hers is the only house in London in which both sexes are served with an equal impartiality.'

'I do not take your meaning.'

'Can you be so artless? Do you intend that you are ignorant of what business is transacted here?'

'By my faith, totally ignorant! Is it not a joinery?'

At that the impudent hussy again snickered, drawing the sheet up to his chin with a languorously importunate movement of his body beneath it, and proceeded to explain to me what the reader, more practised in the ways of the world than a simple country-lad, must have already surmised for himself. My agitation grew as more and more about the trade was revealed to me; but (dare I confess it?) as my agitation grew, so did my interest. If one may earn a competence by doing what often gives one pleasure, why struggle to earn a pittance by doing what

49

often gives one pain? Without either patrimony or patronage, lineage or land, how should either my intelligence or my goodness (on both of which the good parson had often complimented me) raise me above my station? And, no less important, how should such as I, for all the regularity of my features, my bodily strength and my health, aspire to the love of a woman of quality such as Lucy? In his inscrutable design, God had denied me what he had granted to others more fortunate; but as compensation he had given me a greater abundance of one sole commodity than he was like to have accorded to any man else. Should I not be a fool if I were to bury this talent instead of lending it out to Mr Swellington to make from it what he could for me? Such were the the thoughts that Harriet's (or Harry's) disquisition first adumbrated; such those that defined themselves as I performed my matutinal duties in the jakes.

Anon the old woman arrived with a tray and some chocolate, drawing back the heavy curtains, telling us that it was a fine October morning and asking if we had enjoyed good repose. She added that Samuel had given so deep a satisfaction to Lady This that she had sent a messenger to say that she would be retaining him for another night while his Lordship was on business in the West Country. That Harriet's arm should be around my neck (something that I did not desire but that I did not wish to repudiate for fear of checking the flow of her narrative) did not seem to trouble the beldame one whit.

As we sipped the delicious concoction, I minded me of Harriet's reference to one Fanny Hill and asked him about her. Harriet pulled a face, as though the chocolate were quinine, and told me a tale that left me in no doubt that this Fanny Hill was the selfsame jade who had fled from the home of my foster-parents before ever I had got there, to make her way to London in search of her fortune.

It seemed that she had been taken in first by one Mrs Croft and then by one Mrs Rose, the former teaching her all the tricks and stratagems of the trade that she was later to ply so diligently and the latter introducing her to a clientele of the highest quality. Both women had been friends of Mrs Swellington and both, harassed on the one hand by a gang of ruffians eager to usurp their business and on the other hand by dissenters, bigots, puritans, whitehasses, quakers and such like, some of them themselves reformed rakes or rigs and all determined to deny to others the pleasures that they themselves could not or would not enjoy, had fallen into a decay of fortune and had then deceased. Meanwhile, this Fanny Hill had attached herself to a fond old man, too much enfeebled by age and ill-health to make frequent demand on her of the favours that she had so willingly lavished on others far less generous; but the necessity of escorting her to routs, balls, the theatre and the opera, combined with the effort of proving his waning manhood to her, had so hastened his decline that within a few months she was rid of him. To the hurt and astonishment of his excellent brother and sister, good people in far from affluent circumstances, this Fanny Hill had been named in the testament as his sole heiress. There were whispers that the little minx had brought pressures to bear on him in order to achieve this end, threatening to deny him any use of her person unless he so ensured her subsequent felicity, and brother and sister had contemplated a resort to the law. But from such a step they were restrained by a fear of scandal to the family honour.

Once possessed of estates and liberal money in the funds, Fanny Hill hunted down the young blade, now an aging and impoverished ne'er-do-well, with whom she had been initiated into the rites of Venus many a year before and, though he was much reluctant to exchange a state of indigent freedom for one of affluent slavery, she prevailed on him to offer her his hand, no longer having much desire for any other part of the male anatomy. The two of them, settled in the country, had then bred mightily. Fanny had become a veritable martinet, turning one of her daughters out into the streets, to ply her mother's former trade, because she had become big with child by a neighbouring butcher's boy; and despatching a son to the Indies, where he soon expired of a fever, because of the pleasure he took in reading curious and uncommon books. Much of her time was now spent in taking broth and bibles to those less fortunately placed than herself; in invoking all the rigours of the law on those who attempted to profit from the frailties of which she had purged herself; and on keeping a strict surveillance on her spouse, whom she knew, from her own experience, to be a man who liked to make frequent change of mount in the chase. Such a picture of a former devotee of Vice seeking to mask herself behind a veil impudently smuggled from the shrine of Virtue could not but fill me with disgust; the more so since in her new affluence, this paragon of goodness had evidently been too ashamed of her humble origins ever to seek out her parents and help to alleviate their lot.

This narrative concluded, I expressed to Harriet my fear that Mr Swellington might himself demand from me some dalliance. How much harder it would be to oblige one so rugose and raddled than this admittedly comely boy, with his milk-white skin! But Harriet allayed all apprehension, telling me that Mr Swellington achieved the fulfilment of delight not in the arms of any man or woman but merely in the act of impersonation. Straitlacing was more exquisite a torment and delight to him than any embrace; French heels raised him to a higher degree of felicity than any titillation; the touch of silk or velvet on his skin thrilled him more than any human hand; and the full diapason of happiness peeled out for him not on any organ but at the mere twanging of a garter.

'But will he not suffer annoyance if I refuse to accommodate the male sort of client?' I pursued, my fears still not fully allayed on this score. But my companion assured me that Mr Swellington was the most complaisant of ladies and that he would certainly not drive me into any hole into which I did not wish to enter.

Finally, I asked of the third of my fellows, lying sick in

his chamber. 'It must be put about,' replied Harriet, 'for the good name of this house, that he has succumbed to a quaternary fever, since such quality as resort hither are abnormally apprehensive both for their health and for their good names with their spouses. But the truth is that he has a dose of the clap.'

'The clap?' In my innocence I had never heard this word. 'Is that some malady akin to the measles?'

My companion gave his engaging snicker. 'As about as akin as a woman's fount of pleasure to a fig.' He went on to explain to me how this sentimental fellow, William or Bill by name, known to the clients as Sweet William, had conceived what he imagined to be a true love, totally different from his dissembling with ladies of quality, for some trull who worked in a pothouse in Houndsditch. He had been convinced that his Hetty was a model of purity and prudence; but when the fire of his love had started to scald a passage through him, he had suffered a fit of melancholy almost as cruel as his malady. A leech, proficient in such matters, had subjected him to the most cruel of torments and it was to be hoped that he was now on the way to mending.

At this Harriet jumped, fully naked, out of bed, and reached for a robe of figured silk, into which he passed arms that surpassed for whiteness and smoothness those of many a wench. 'Ah me!' he sighed. 'You have given me a night to remember. But remembered joy has in it as much bitterness as sweetness.'

Thinking of my lost beloved, I could not but agree with him.

3

Some two hours later I was summoned to Mr Swellington's presence, where you could never imagine such a display of unguents, liniments, salves, pomades, ointments, lacquers, paints, powders, patches and perfumes all gathered in a single chamber. He was *in puris naturalibus* but for a robe thrown over his shoulders and some knickers edged with the finest Brussels lace. Having asked me if I had slept well and were now fully rested (at this he darted a knowing look at Harriet, who was already in the room), he informed me that he had a duty for me to perform. My first surmise was that some client had either arrived earlier than expected or had sent round some minion with an order demanding speedy fulfilment; but he went on to explain: 'I observed yesterday the way in which you stole surreptitious glances at the hair of my bosom and indeed of other portions of my anatomy. You were right. A proper lady cannot take too much care of her appearance. The Duchess of W——— is the laughing stock of the Palace of St James's for the hair on her upper lip. How much more shall I be the laughing stock of the Parish of Westminster for the hair in places less conspicuous but even more unexpected! Good Madame Sosostris, who provides me with the wherewithal to maintain my beauty in its pristine state – ' he here waved an arm in the direction of the shelves loaded with bottles, boxes and jars – 'has but recently had brought over from Paris a certain concoction of wax, asafoetida and who knows what else, that is, so she assures me, the most efficacious depilatory that the wit of man ever devised. Even now our good Harriet is making it

54

hot for us. I should wish no hands other than yours to apply it.'

I pleaded that I was totally unused to such a task but he would hear none of it. Harriet then brought to me the most evil-smelling brew that it were possible to imagine, indeed like glue such as a joiner might use, still steaming in the skillet. This I applied to Mr Swellington on his directions, making him emit the most fearful screams, as of a woman in the throes of a difficult labour, each time that it touched his skin. 'Ah, I faint! I die! Ah! Ah! Ah!' he would bawl, then breaking off to chide me: 'Do not hesitate, boy! If the preparation be not applied when it is steaming, then it is applied in vain.' Once that he was covered with the malodorous stuff, he jigged about the room, for all the world as if he had succumbed to an attack of St Elmo's Fire, until it had hardened about him, black and shiny, like the carapace of a cockroach. Then he lay out on the bed and told me that I must needs chip and tug it off. I shrank from this duty but he told me briskly: 'Come, boy! Do not hesitate! Tonight we expect company, and not only must I appear at my most winsome for it, but I have much to put in hand in preparation.' At that I set to, while Harriet stood in the doorway, looking on. As each upstanding hair was tugged away with the wax, the poor fretful porpentine let out cry on cry, imploring every Christian saint and every pagan deity to rescue him from his torment. Yet it was easy to see that he also took delight in the business, as he bawled out: 'Oh, what a delectable distress, oh, what a poignant pleasure! What a treasure of a torturer! Like the bee, you are a source of both sweetness and sting!' When I had done, he admired my handiwork in the pier-glass set up in the centre of the room with evident satisfaction, even though he had the appearance of having just been boiled alive. 'Madame Sosostris indeed knows her trade, as you do also, sweetheart,' he declared.

Somewhat pigeon-hearted at the thought of the company that might be expected and of the duties that might be required of me, despite all Harriet's assurances, I now ventured to question Mr Swellington on this matter, to be told that tonight it would be a night for the ladies and tomorrow for the gentlemen. The gentlemen, he added, were more docile and more proper; but the ladies were more generous. 'Many a gentleman,' he said, 'will bargain here with all the tenacity of his own housekeeper purchasing a cock for dinner in Berwick Market. The ladies do not bargain; but even the richest of them will sometimes ask for credit and then must needs be dunned, as though I were any trading tailor or cobbler.'

'As for tonight,' I declared, 'you may count on my services. I do not doubt that I shall rise to the occasion to the satisfaction both of yourself and of any customer whom you put in my way. But for the night following, I must beg you to excuse me. I am like one who has drunk coffee all his life and whom a dish of chocolate will only make spew.'

'Good Harriet here has already informed me of your predilection. But just as he who has been brought up in penury to subsist on only gruel may one day learn the pleasures of eating grouse, it is not impossible that your taste may change.'

'I doubt it, sir.'

'*Madam* – if you please!' At that he gave me a smart rap with the hair-brush with which he was engaged in teasing that monument of a wig. 'If Harriet is to be believed, it seems you did not serve the wench ill last night in bed.'

'I was swept away on the full tide of passion and hardly knew where I was cast up.'

'The tide returns regularly and no doubt it will return again soon. But no matter for the moment. Sam will, I hope, have come back by tomorrow, with his pockets filled and his reservoirs not entirely empty and he will play his part. Eleven years at the mast robs a man of any niceness, even more effectively than the same period in a monastery. He takes what is coming and comes in what it takes. Alas, he will be absent tonight, which may put an extra burden or two on you – or under you. However some of my irregulars have already promised to appear and Harriet shall shortly go forth to arrange for more.'

When I questioned him about these irregulars, he told me that many were foot-guards or horse-guards, who eked out their meagre shillings with a guinea or half-guinea. 'They are a rascally lot, given to intemperance and thievery, and for that reason it is best if I retain any monies on your account in my strong-box. Many is the time that one of them has made off with some object of virtue as additional recompense for his performance of vice; and many is the gentleman who has bewailed the loss of a fob-watch or a purse and many the lady who has bewailed the loss of a ring or a pendant.' Those irregulars who were not of the service were, for the most part, of better quality, being scriveners, shopkeepers, watermen, errand-boys and such like. One was a sprig of the nobility – 'A darling boy,' Mr Swellington went on. 'He can only take pleasure in the act of darkness if he receives some monetary recompense, however small. The human heart is strange and no man, however clever, can plumb its whys and wherefores.'

You never saw such a motley crew as these irregulars. Some were indeed handsome fellows, with their country complexions, their brawny limbs and their bold and frank features. Others were pockmarked and impetiginous, uncombed and unscoured, their boots reeky and their finger-nails so black that one could only suppose that they had been scratching their own grimy skins. While he was talking with these, I observed that Mr Swellington sniffed all the time at a pomander. One or two newcomers were bashful and ill at ease; but one betrayed his excitement at the propsect before him with such an obviousness that Mr Swellington whispered to me that he feared that the glass might be spilled before ever it reached the lips for which it was destined. The sprig of the nobility, instead of being dressed in the height of fashion as I had supposed, was wearing jerkin and torn breeches, such as one might

57

see on the most common of day-labourers, and talked with the tones of such a person. The buffet was loaded with viands and wines and Mr Swellington had to urge the soldiers on more than one occasion to refrain from approaching it until the arrival of the ladies.

I had imagined that such ladies as would attend would be those already in the sere and yellow leaf, their wells dry and the area around those wells cracked and shrunken. Some indeed were so; but many were both young and beauteous, having been driven to Mr Swellington's for a variety of reasons: their husbands' preference for the pleasures of the gaming-tables over those of the matrimonial couch, their infidelities, their impotences, their absences. Sometimes the reason lay not with the husband but with the wife who, wearying of the same repast day after day, wished for some new savour to titillate her jaded palate. What astonished me was how often the freshest and loveliest rose would prepare to twine herself around the grimiest and most crooked of stakes; whereas the bloom that was on the point of shedding its petals or had indeed already done so would attach itself to one stalwart and straight. I feared for myself, imagining that I should have to solace this or that slouching scarecrow, hulky harridan or evil-favoured hag. What was my joy therefore when Mr Swellington led up a girl of some seventeen or eighteen summers, dressed all in widow's weeds and introduced her to me as My Lady V———, but lately bereft of her husband who had been drowned off the coast of Bermuda while sailing thither to visit a property. 'She has come hither for some consolation for her grief,' Mr Swellington informed me. 'Have you not, dear child?' For answer, a single tear ran down her downcast cheek. 'She has no taste for the revelry that is now going forward here' – already, indeed, the company was becoming far from decorous, with many an ancient beldame astraddle an ensign's knee and many a martial tongue preparing to sound reveille on something other than the bugle – 'and I therefore propose to you that you should take her to your chamber, there to converse with her in peace. Harriet has set out some comfits and a jug of ratafee.'

I did not need to be bid twice; but my fair companion hung back, seemingly reluctant, so that I must needs draw her along by the hand. As we mounted the stairs, she told me between sobs that her husband had been such a good man, such a handsome man, one likely to win great fame in the country. What compensation, she asked, was a great fortune for the loss of such a one? When we entered the chamber, the tears were running fast down her cheeks, their deepened carnation going off exquisitely into the hue of glazed snow. I was reluctant to obtrude on such grief and could do no more than sit on the bed beside her, holding her hand and attempting to console her. In doing so, I reminded her that the Good Book had promised us that the Lord defendeth the fatherless and the widow; that He is the resurrection and the life; and that He gives light to them that sit in darkness and in the shadow of death. To all this she listened still in tears and still with her hand clasped in mine. Then she looked up and in the most dulcet tones imaginable said: 'And the Good Book also tells us that they that sow in tears, shall reap in joy. Is it not so, Danny?' I nodded. She jumped up off the bed, and cried out at that: 'Then let us sow that we may reap!' She went over to the dressing-table, unloosing her raven hair the time, and picked up something from it: 'But let us not be too literal about such reaping. You needs must wear this.' I then saw that she was holding out to me one of the satchels that I had supposed to be for the sale of lavender when I had seen the old hag of a cook stitching them and had never supposed to be for the retention of quite another sort of seed. I stammered, all confused, that I did not catch her drift and she then replied, 'Ah, Danny, how innocent you are! Can it be possible! I have always wished to initiate a virgin into the rites of Paphos.' I forbore to mention that I was not a virgin and merely smiled bashfully upon her. 'Dear, dear Danny!' She kissed me, full on the lips, the tears tasting salt on them, and then bade me make haste, repeating yet again that never before had she had the good fortune to make love with a virgin, not even with her husband, now deceased, on her wedding-night.

In a trice, she had stripped off her widow's weeds, throwing them all pell-mell on the floor and stood before me in all her beauty, no longer bashful but brazen. Her faced amazed me for the exquisiteness of its shape; nor could I help admiring her two ripe enchanting breasts finely plumped out in flesh, so firm that they sustained themselves in scorn of any stays; then their nipples, pointing different ways, here left, there right, to mask their pleasing separation; and then, most enticing of all, the delicious tract of the belly which terminated in a parting or rift scarce discernible, that modestly seemed to retire downwards and seek shelter between two plump fleshy thighs, while the curling hair that overspread its delightful front clothed it with the richest sable fur in the universe. In short, she was evidently a subject for the painters to court her sitting to them for a pattern of female beauty, in all the true pride and pomp of her nakedness.

She gasped – whether with fear, amazement, delight or some admixture of all three, I know not – when she witnessed my grand oak-tree rising out of its thicket; then she threw herself upon me, in an exultant fury, and the two of us toppled over on to her widow weeds. Recking nothing of them, she spread her thighs wide, to discover between them the mark of her sex, that red-centred cleft whose lips, vermilioning inwards, expressed a rubid line such as Rubens's touch of colouring could never attain to the life and delicacy. Reaching for the satchel, she instructed me in its use with evident pleasure.

Our business concluded, she must all at once begin to sob with, 'Oh, my poor dear husband!' 'My good husband!' 'Such a husband never before existed in the world nor shall ever exist again!' as she accoutred herself in her weeds. 'Danny!' she cried, 'how could you have obliged me to do anything so monstrous and unnatural? I did but come up for a few moments of comfort.'

'And I trust you will come up again for the same purpose,' I rejoindered.

'Oh, Danny, Danny, Danny!'

At that she slipped away by the back-staircase, bidding me not to follow her. I learned later that the old cook was seated at the door and that it was to her that the weeping widow made over her bounty, which in due turn was handed to Mr Swellington.

Like some stately galleon tossed on the high seas, the whole noble house was now rocking and reeling in a universal tempest of passion. From the rooms above, to which I had never penetrated, came sighs, groans, moans, grunts and ululations. Briefly, looking upwards, I saw a part of a well-shaped leg and the flash of a naked thigh between the boots of hussar, but then, with merry laughter and a scampering, the vision was lost to me. A moment later petticoats came billowing down the stairwell, covering my face and shoulders. I extricated myself from this pleasing form of mantrap, smelling the heady musk with which the silk was saturated, and proceeded downwards, where, on the last step but one, I found Harriet seated, alone and disconsolate, his face in his hands and his skirts rucked above his knees in a most unladylike manner. 'You do not join in the revelry?' I asked.

'There is nought of revelry here for me,' he rejoined in a sulky tone, pursing his lips and tossing his head. 'Truly it is a disgusting spectacle, well-born ladies, ladies of quality behaving like the bitches in the highways. And these men – they are like maddened dogs in pursuit of those bitches' malodorous privates. No shame, no modesty! I tried to converse with one young blade, the one that demands money even though his father is a Croesus, but he would have none of it! You will see, tomorrow will be greatly different.'

'*Cras amet qui nunquam amavit!*' I said, giving him a playful pat on the cheek. But the poor wretch evidently wanted for any education, for he merely turned aside his head and sulkily muttered under his breath something inaudible to me.

In the main room the revelry was at its height, presenting such a scene that would have rivalled the orgies of Babylon. One of the footguards, accoutred in nought but his belt, was belabouring the shrivelled buttocks of an ancient beldame with the side of his sword; a horse-guard was riding another, pricking her sides with his spurs (all that he wore apart from his bearskin) as she bore him about the room, from time to time emitting a piercing whinny; two ladies were, to my amazement, engaged in an exchange so intimate that I needs must look away. In the middle of the chamber, a number of the revellers were circled in what (if I may be allowed so far-fetched an metaphor) most resembled a human daisy-chain with Mr Swellington, wig all askew and bodice all unlaced, cracking a whip at the hub. Guido, being unable to produce any more substantial evidence of his admiration, was giving tongue to some young lady who could not have been of more than sixteen or seventeen summers. On the threshold, blocking my path so that I need must step over him, Sam lay sprawled with who knows how many ladies sprawled atop and about him. For a reason obscure to me, unless it were because of his former estate as a tar, they were calling him 'Jolly Roger' as they kissed and caressed him mightily.

'Danny!' Mr Swellington cried out, with a crack of the whip, as soon as he set eyes on me. And, 'Danny!' all the ladies took up, disjointing themselves from their company, rising from the chairs, the sofas and the floor, tripping over each other, thrusting each other aside, pushing and pulling, for all the world like starved Hibernian peasants fighting over a last potato. In a trice they were on top of me, tearing at my finery, with a ripping of silk and a dissevering of damask, and I fell backwards, another Orpheus, into the arms of some brawny Maenad. Let me pass over what then befell me, merely stating that in the whole history of human congress, never can one man have given so much for so many, to cries of, 'Lawks!', 'Lord-love-a-duck!', 'Did you ever!', ' 'Tis a veritable monster!'

and such like, that would have brought a blush to my cheek were that cheek not so firmly pressed to a cheek yet more shapely and far larger belonging to the maiden astride me. It is likely that I should have expired from this too much of bliss, had not Mr Swellington at last called the rout to order, with cries of, 'Order! Order! Ladies! Please!', his whip cracking as he set about those who would not or could not desist despite his commands. 'It is ill-mannered not merely to empty the dish but to attempt to lick the last fragment from it. There will be other such feasts but now I beg you have done!'

Such was the climax of this night of boisterous pleasure and indeed I was aching in every fibre of my being as I at last struggled to my feet. The ladies began to re-assemble their clothes and to repair the ravages inflicted on their coiffures and their complexions. The gentlemen, having dressed themselves far more speedily, resorted to the buffet, where they poured themselves great quantities of drink. Mr Swellington was manifestly displeased at the spectacle of his best Rhenish and Bordeaux wines being drunk as though they were the cheapest of ales in a pot-house and went along to the gentlemen in an effort to dissuade them.

On a sudden two of the ladies, whom I had but lately seen asprawl about Sam, were tugging at each other's hair, scratching and spitting at each other, like two tiger-cats, and Mr Swellington must needs leave his care of the wine to separate them. 'Ladies! Decorum! Decorum!'

They were certainly two most delectable morsels, each young and with eyes aflash and white teeth bared in the access of their mutual fury. 'Trull!' 'Chippy!' 'Minx!' 'Slut!' 'Skit!' 'Punk!' Never had I thought to hear words, such as I blush to transcribe here, issuing from the mouths of members of the fairer and weaker sex, much less from two such high-born ladies.

Mr Swellington clapped his hands over his ears, as appalled as I. 'Ladies! *Ladies!*' At that, conscious at last of the shame of such language, they drew themselves up, with an agitation of their fans and a quivering of their petticoats, their necks a delightful carmine and their eyes still flashing.

'Madam,' said one, with a dignity greatly at odds with her former abandonment of all dignity, 'tomorrow my seconds will await on you.'

'Much obliged, madam,' said the other, curtseying in the most sardonic manner imaginable. At that they swept from the room, Mr Swellington hurrying after them to relieve them (as I learned later) of their fees for the night's entertainment.

'Ladies first' was indeed the rule of the house for first must Mr Swellington collect the plunder and then must he distribute it among the stallions. As the last carriage clattered over the cobbles and as the last chair, bearing its overwearied burden back to some lordly or even ducal mansion, swayed out into the dawn of yet another day, the gentlemen crowded about Mr Swellington, paying little attention to his exhortation, 'One at a time! One at a time, please!' This one complained that he had received recompense too scant for such an abundance of sport; that one that Mr Swellington was falling short of his promises; that other that he needs must have another guinea, since his shrew of a wife would otherwise berate and belabour him for his absence the whole livelong night. Seated at a table in the hall, Mr Swellington excited my admiration with his judiciousness and calm. When one ruffian became over insistent, he reminded him that if one shakes a tree too hard, then it may never again yield fruit. At last, with much glowering and grouching, much pouting and crabbing, the company dispersed. Some were informed that on the morrow they would be expected for a different kind of diversion, a prospect that elicited more groans than glee.

'Law! I am quite spent!' Mr Swellington sighed, collapsing on to a sofa, bespilled with wine and other liquids intoxicating to the ladies, throwing off his wig and loosening his bodice yet further. 'But 'twas a merry party!'

'If you are spent, in what case am I?' I asked.

'Harriet, you took not the smallest part in our revels.'

'I abhor such behaviour,' rejoined the minx. 'These are not ladies but the veritable scourings of the gutters.'

Sam (or Jolly Roger as I needs must now think of him) snored loudly in a corner, his breeches still undone and his open shirt revealing a tattooed serpent twining among the ample undergrowth on his manly chest.

'Yes, 'twas a good night's work! And I mean not only in guineas,' Mr Swellington went on. 'This is indeed a joiner's shop, for it is we and such as we that keep joined what might otherwise fall apart; that maintain the marital bed in good repair; that fend off the inroads of the beetle and the worm.'

'What paradox is this?' I asked, much amazed.

'No paradox. Were it not for my house, where ladies such as these may find a temporary diversion, they might seek out for themselves liaisons more permanent, to the detriment of their marriage vows, their spouses and their issue. Here, when the craving for variety takes them, they may sate the capricious appetite of a moment with the feast of a moment at no great loss in money and no loss at all in any other particular.' Mr Swellington refilled his beaker with ratafee, quaffed from it and continued: 'When we observe a woman grown contrary, ill-humoured, splenetic or melancholic, plagued by the megrims or the vapours, it is usually either because she has wearied of the pleasure that her husband can accord her or because her husband but rarely accords her any pleasure at all. Such women grow shrewish with their spouses, tittle-tattle about each other, espouse all kinds of absurd and danger-ous causes, scold their children, castigate their servants, and live in a constant state of exacerbation or dejection. They become like locks grown rusty for lack of oiling and so incapable of yielding up the treasures safeguarded within. But let the balsamic fluid but creep into every cranny and crevice and the wards at once are loosened. I am therefore not only a benefactress to myself and to

65

those in my employ, but also to the whole of womankind and the human race at large.'

Sam emitted a particularly deafening snore at the end of this speech, as though in approbation.

'Well, to bed!' cried Mr Swellington, leaping to his feet. 'Tomorrow we must have the roses in our cheeks, so that we may enjoy another such night of pleasure.'

'And what of the duel?' I asked, fearful that one of such two beautiful damsels might ere long be slain.

'Take no thought of it! I shall conduct you to it, on the day after tomorrow – indeed, after tomorrow's rout. You will find it mightily diverting.'

'I doubt if I shall be one of your party,' Harriet pouted. 'In former times women knew their place and such houses as this were only for the stronger sex.'

'*Tempora mutantur et nos mutamur in illis*,' Mr Swellington rejoined, surprising me by this erudition. 'Come, girl! Help me to bed!' He yawned vastly. 'Lawks, but I must be the most tired lass in the whole world this dawn.'

Sam continued to snore.

4

Forgetting Mr Swellington's comparisons, I had expected that our revels of the night that followed would, if that were possible, be even more riotous than those that had gone before, since women are notoriously more delicate, timorous and fastidious than men. What was my surprise, therefore, to find such sobriety and reserve of behaviour that I might have been, not in a house of pleasure, but in some St James's Club. Even the irregulars talked in lowered voices, with attempts, often ludicrous, to imitate the accents and to adopt the vocabulary of their betters. Here was no overloaded buffet and no swilling of spirituous liquors as though they were water. Here a little group passed round a decanter of port; here two sat demurely, each sipping at a glass of madeira; here the Lord High Chancellor and some eminent advocates asked Harriet if she might prepare them a dish of tea. The cakes were small and plain and were nibbled rather than eaten, with much sweeping away of crumbs with languid hands or faintly perfumed kerchiefs.

As I passed about the room, being introduced by Mr Swellington to My Lord This and My Sir Something That, I noticed that many of those present were not of the quality at all but were palpably clerks, shopkeepers, tradesmen and suchlike. I remarked on this privately to my master (who was gowned with much less than his usual extravagance and wore but a single choker of diamonds) to be told: 'This, Danny, is a freemasonry in which all men are equal while they are being their true selves. Tomorrow the Lord Chancellor will speak in peremptory manner to the scrivener who is too slow to indite some deed; tonight he is raising his glass to him. Tomorrow that foolish coxcomb over there will berate his barber for having nicked his hardly-existent chin; tonight he is handing him a slice of madeira cake. That admiral over there, with the purple wattles, might well order our Sam fifty lashes if he were still before the mast; tonight he is asking him the source and meaning of those curious diagrams that he bears inscribed, like scars, on his weather-worn vellum. This is indeed a Beloved Republic, where no man is of greater degree than another, no man takes precedence over another, and where each gives according to his abilities and takes according to his needs.'

I was curious to learn what were the topics of the conversations that were being carried on in such hushed tones around me and, to this end, went about the company with a dish of biscuits in my hand. As I passed a Lord Bishop, I heard him say, ' T'was such a cock –'; but on my appearing before him, he continued 'and bull story, my dear,' thus greatly disappointing me. Three young fellows, dressed in the height of fashion, were commenting critically on the apparel of all those in the room, saying that the cut of the breeches of such a one was mightily indiscreet; that this other one must have had resort to a stall in the Petticoat Lane for such a villainous cravat; that the shoes of my Lord Bishop were so much worn down in the heels that it were no wonder that he complained so frequently of the gout. A portly gentleman with a red face was discussing in confidential tone what I assumed to be affairs of state with another gentleman so yellow, wilting and thin that he most resembled a melting tallow candle. Imagine my astonishment when, approaching near to them, I heard: 'A mere minim of sweet basil – a very cantlet – will do wonders for the dish.' Was it possible that two such worthy-looking gentlemen were merely common cooks?

Gradually and decorously each Jill found his Jack. I had long been aware that I had been an object of curiosity and attention to a number of the company, who stole as many covert glances at my breeches as at my face. More than one, indeed, invited me to sit with him; but I excused myself by saying that I must needs help out Mrs Swellington (I was careful to accord him the Mrs in company) with the disposition of beverages. Finally one, whom I later learned to be nabob but recently returned from the East Indies, approached my master and, raising a hand but talking so loud behind it that I could hear his every word, asked if the young lad over there (myself) were available. I trembled for what answer Mr Swellington might give, for, whereas Harriet was no bad semblance of a maid except for one, certainly most important particular, this bloated and gibbous mass, as bald as any coot, was nothing to my taste. To my relief Mr Swellington answered him: 'Alas, the poor boy has pulled his riding-muscle and will be of no service to anyone this night. But I have here a jolly gypsy, as honest as the day is long and as long as he is honest, who will serve you mightily well instead.'

Two by two, like the animals entering the ark, the gentlemen made their way up the staircase, their voices lowered and their expressions sombre. Sometimes the two was a three and, on one occasion, even a four. Harriet, all rustling flounces and glittering jewels and no longer accoutred in her usual sober maid's attire, was supporting a gentleman so elderly that he could scarce lift one swollen foot from one stair up to the next. Sam, in his sailor's gear, had a young blade on either tattooed arm, for all the world like some jolly jack-tar back in port after many weeks of abstinence. He whispered something to Mr Swellington about goose-grease and rods; to which our master replied that both had been laid ready by Harriet in the chamber.

When Mr Swellington and I were alone, he said to me: 'Now, Danny, do you wish to see some sport?'

'What sport, ma'am?' I asked, remembering that I must so address him and not as 'sir'.

'The most comical sport in the world. Come with me!' I followed where he beckoned, up the stairs and into what

I had thought to be a closet. 'I had this glass, most cunningly devised, sent to me from Murano, near to Venice, at great cost. Those of my gentlemen who gaze through it must pay dearly for that privilege; but since I affect you greatly and since you are one of the household, you shall look for nothing.' It was indeed like some magic glass, devised by a wizard, for though we could look through it, to those on its other side it appeared to be no more than a mirror. Mr Swellington placed a finger on his painted lips, enjoining me to silence, and then slid a panel sideways high above our heads, so that we could not only see but also hear what was passing. Indeed, it was the most strange and ridiculous spectacle that ever I did witness.

There was the Lord Chancellor, lying on the ground, a formless lump of blue-veined blubber, in nought but his socks and his wig, this last full-bottomed like its wearer. Astride him stood just such a lanky, murderous, blue-jowled ruffian as he must often have despatched to the plantations or the gallows. 'Yes, yes, yes!' cries out My Lord, as though begging for the mercy that he has so often denied to others. 'Please! I pray you! Now! Yes!' Then like Zeus descending to Danae in a golden shower, so the rogue descends to him; but unlike Danae, My Lord receives the benison, not between his thighs, but full in the face. Such a comical fluttering of the eyelids, heaving like a stranded whale and gulping and gurgling you never did see! I could hardly restrain myself from laughing out aloud and so betraying our presence. 'This is gold, gold, gold!' cries out My Lord. 'This is gold to me!'

'And gold must be paid for with gold,' retorts the ruffian, Mr Swellington nodding vigorously in agreement besides me.

'For such as you, the wages of sin should be death,' My Lord mumbles, rising now to his feet and reaching for a cloth. 'But no matter.' His former ecstasy had now been succeeded by just such a displacency, even spinosity that he so often exhibited on the Bench. Having eaten of the banquet, it now seemed to lie ill on his stomach. 'Despatch! Despatch!' he shouted at the rascal. 'Away! I shall pay the account with good Mrs Swellington in due course!' The other quickly dressed himself, with many a 'If Your Lordship will excuse me',' As Your Lordships wills', 'If I do not incommode Your Lordship' – this last as he pulls a grimy and tattered hose out from under His Lordship's naked hams as he sits slouched, all in a melancholy sulk, on the bed.

When the ruffian had at last left the room, His Lordship rose wearily from the bed, with many a grunt and sigh, and began to dress himself. I was about to quit the closet but Mr Swellington restrained me, placing a hand on my arm. 'There will be more fun yet, if I am not mistaken. Wait, Danny!' We waited, while His Lordship pulled up his hose, put on his shirt and drew on his breeches, still with many a sigh and groan. Then he approached the mirror to tie his cravat. Forgetting that he could not see us because of the cunning of those Italian glass-blowers, I again must needs be checked from retreating by Mr Swellington's hands on my arm. Having tied his cravat, His Lordship went on staring at his own reflection, and also staring, though he did not know it, into my eyes; and as he stared, with the most woebegone expression you ever saw, he murmured to himself: 'Ah God, God, God! Would that I might be hanged by the neck like many such a poor rogue that I have despatched to the gallows!' Mr Swellington thought this more diverting than anything else that had passed heretofore and needs must put a hand over his mouth to choke his laughter. But I felt a strange sadness and heaviness of the spirits, even though I knew that His Lordship was the most pompous and proud old fool in Christendom.

Omne animale post coitum triste; and though no other gentleman was as melancholic as His Lordship, each was in no manner gay as he came down the stairs, but all sober, grave and even mumpish. They were now quick to take their leave but not always quick to pay their dues.

To one, who was making his excuses that he was awaiting the return of some ship of his, I heard Mr Swellington reply with some tartness that if the flow of cash were dammed, then so must also be the flow of vital fluids, adding, 'I hope that your cargo may soon be unloaded, for else no cargo can be unloaded for you in this house.' I marvelled at his tenacity and courage with people of such standing and moment, who might with a word have his throat slit on a dark night, his visage marred, his house put to the fire or his own self despatched on a convict hulk to the Americas. But Mr Swellington explained the matter to me: 'For such as these, I am dung. But the exotic fruits that they crave cannot grow unless that dung is there to feed it. The dung may seem to them defiling but they well know its worth.'

Sam now came down the stairs, his two young blades once again on either arm, but now they could hardly walk, so painful was it to them. 'I can see that Sam has led you a merry dance,' Mr Swellington observed.

'Indeed, yes, ma'am,' replied one of the two, rubbing his posterior. 'We have expiated all our misdeeds for at least a week.'

When the gentleman had left us and the last of the irregulars had been paid his due (each again arguing much and protesting that he had never been recompensed so poorly for such a hard night's work), Mr Swellington asked me if I were tired or if I wished to see the duel between the two ladies, that would take place that very dawn in a glade in Richmond Forest. 'I have done nought this night to weary me, ma'am,' I replied. 'Good!' he exclaimed. 'Then you will see some wondrous sport. Sam is mightily fatigued from his exertions with rod and line but Harriet will accompany us, as will Guido and that poor wretch, John, who has been in his chamber this last week, now weeping out his heart for that faithless trull of his and now passing burning bodkins.'

This John was such a mild-mannered, ordinary-looking lad, such as you might see behind a counter in a haberdasher's, matching buttons or thread, that I wondered both how he had got himself into a trade such as ours and what use he might be at it. But Mr Swellington explained to me that, whereas Guido was wondrous mellifluous with his tongue, so was this lad wondrous adroit with his fingers, coaxing out the most recondite harmonies from any organ you might give him to play. Now, as he sat opposite to me in the coach, he spoke not at all but merely heaved one sigh on another; but whether these were for what he had lost of for what he had gained I knew not. Harriet did nothing but babble throughout the journey – his gentleman, decrepit to my eyes, had been the handsomest, most vigorous, most commanding, most thrustful gentleman that ever you could wish for – when all at once he fell silent at the sound of galloping horses behind us. Mr Swellington clutched my arm and poor John for a moment ceased his sighing. We were then, in the hour just before the dawn, in a darksome lane near the Palace of Kew, and our coachman was reining in the horses. A pistol all at once came through the window and a voice bade us, 'Stand and deliver!' The tone was peremptory, yet the voice itself was marvellous high, as of a boy or a woman.

''Tis Mad, Bad Bess!' Mr Swellington hissed at me. Then he called out: 'There is someone inside here that will stand higher than any other and deliver more than any other!'

'Who is this paragon?' demanded this Bess, in a voice in no way grown more tender.

'He is one Danny Hill; and the like you have never seen before.' Then, 'Go out from the coach, Danny!' he whispered to me. 'Show her! Else all we have here is lost!' And at that he hurriedly began to remove his rings, brooches and necklaces and to shove them down the happy valley.

Somewhat loath, I got out of the coach, but when I saw the hussy who was still pointing her pistol at me, I felt an instant enthusiasm rise so strong that I could hardly walk for it. True, I could not see this Bess's face but for its snow-white forehead, lambent in the first light of day, and its

73

lustrous eyes, since a scarf shielded all the lower half; but the form, in breeches and jerkin, was exquisite on the champing steed. 'You spoke right, beldame!' she exclaimed, slipping down off the horse and affixing its reins to a tree. Then, perhaps fearing some trick, she shouted out: 'But if you move, coachman, then I shall blow off this pretty gentleman's head with no compunction.' At that she begins to lower her breeches with one hand, while with the other she still holds the gun at my head. Then all at once the gun is pointing at a place even more vulnerable and I am in such a sweat of fever, as much now for my manhood as previously for my life, that I wonder if the shrinking of my spirit may not be the prefiguration of another kind of shrinking. But no sooner do I see her wondrous thighs glimmering in the first auroral blush than I have no thought of pistol, imminent death or a fate similar to Guido's but at once set myself to my task with a will, all unawares that Mr Swellington, John and Harriet are gazing out of the window, agog and aghast at one and the same moment, and that the coachman and Guido are looking down from the box, the former hardly able to contain himself and the other devoutly wishing that he had something to contain.

When I had finished my task, the hussy was once again on her horse in a trice, shouting out, 'Yes, verily you spake right, old beldame!' as she swerved about and made off into the early mist of day.

'You did well, Danny,' Mr Swellington commended me, patting my hands as I once again seated myself beside him on the coach.

'I should have preferred to sip from the beaker rather than drain it at a single gulp,' I answered. 'But I was loath to detain you all too long.'

'You gave that poor jade something to prize above all diamonds or rubies,' Mr Swellington said with a certain smug thankfulness as he now retrieved his jewels from out of happy valley and began to replace them on fingers and bosom.

'I had heard before of the dangers of highwaymen to people of wealth, consequence or quality. But I did not know until now that women could pose the selfsame danger.'

'There are two or three other such wenches as Mad, Bad Bess; and I doubt not that, ere long, there will be many more. This is a world in which (as you observed but this evening) men increasingly assume the qualities of women, and so, inevitably, women must increasingly assume the capacities of men. Mad, Bad Bess is one of the levellers and she would wish to level, not only all degree between high and low and rich and poor, but also all difference between the sexes. But as you witnessed, show but that difference in all its splendour and strength and she becomes its willing slave.'

' 'Twas I that felt like a slave when that pistol was directed at my fountain head.'

Mention of the pistol reminded me of the duel and I asked Mr Swellington what was the preferred weapons of the ladies.

'Men, as you will know, use swords, knives, pistols and such like in their contests with each other; and so it is from these that they must choose when they fight a duel. Women demonstrate their power by other, more subtle means, to achieve the supremacy. Their weapons may be no less dangerous even though at first they seem so in-substantial.'

'And what are their weapons, ma'am?' I asked, puzzled by the drift of all this.

'First – the tongue.'

'The tongue?'

'The sharpest sword that was ever invented: capable of a blast more efficacious than that of any gun; more piercing than any poignard. If such is the weapon chosen, the two ladies may scream whatever malisons, aspersions, execrations, fulminations, scurrilities and anathemata that they may wish (at a distance of twenty paces) until one or the other either falls silent or succumbs to the vapours.'

75

'And the second weapon?'

'The dress. Many a time two booths are set up in some dell for a duel between two ladies. They each then apparel themselves and show off their finery, the one to the other, with many a hissed compliment that is, in truth, no compliment at all, and many an envious look. Each returns to her booth and garbs herself anew. So they continue until, in a frenzy, one or other can no longer contain herself and says what is truly in her mind instead of what she believes ought to be there.'

'And the third weapon?'

'That you will witness for yourself. 'Tis the most potent of all weapons that a woman possesses in order to work her will; and it is that weapon that these two ladies have chosen to use against each other.'

I pressed him to enlighten me further but he would not do so, telling me that I must have patience and I should see such sport as I had never seen before in my life.

When we arrived in the dell, the sun had begun to rise, a fiery orb in the east, dissipating the matutinal mist, and many people, both gentry such as had visited our house in the last two evenings and the common sort, were already present. I saw a number of carriages, their horses cropping the herbage, while their elegant owners, all a-twitter with expectation, walked the dewy sward. An area in the middle had been roped off to form a quadrangle and within this were such a crew of ragamuffins, rapscallions, bully-boys, miscreants and misfits as I had never before seen gathered all together in a single place.

'Who are these runnions here?' I asked Mr Swellington. 'And what are they about?'

'They are the sweepings of the gutter, the gaol and the garret; and it is on them that the two ladies must now prove their power and demonstrate their domination.'

'How so?'

'Each lady will lie out on one of those two couches over there' – at this Mr Swellington pointed to the far end of the glade – 'and spread all her charms. These ruffians must then make a choice between joining the army of the one or the other. In return for his fealty, each man will be accorded something more delectable than the king's shilling. She who rallies the larger army to her cause, is the victrix.'

At that moment the umpire, a massy and red-cheeked gentleman, called out in a stentorian voice: 'Pray silence, ladies and gentlemen. The rules of our contest will be known to all of you. Neither lady must utter any word of seduction or encouragement; and no member of the public may barrack, boo, clap, cheer, disparage, acclaim or give any other demonstration of approbation or disapprobation. All shall be silent; all, save our volunteers, shall be still.' These words were greeted by a sound of applause, which he silenced with the raising of a hand. 'First let the good surgeon step forth, in case either contestant may suffer any detriment or damage.' A gnome-like figure came into view, a bag containing the implements of his profession held in one hand. Again there was applause and again the umpire stilled it. 'And now our two contestants and their seconds!' At that the two wenches stepped forth, each from a tent pitched on either side of the glade and each accompanied by two women, almost as beauteous as herself, as her seconds. One of the contestants was fair, the other dark; and rarely can a day have dawned on two such visions of loveliness at one and the same moment. Each was clad in no more than a shift that seemed to have been woven from cobwebs, so fine was its texture, and some feathered mules; each faced the company boldly, with no bashful lowering of the eyes to escape the gazes fastened on them and no bashful lowering of the hands to conceal what was only too visible, albeit through a veil. Set out on a table beside each couch were glasses, bottles of eau de vie and sal volatile, smelling-salts and a plentiful supply of napkins of the finest Bogside lawn. Each lady threw off her shift and then, helped on to the couch by her two attendant damsels, spread wide her thighs to give us a full view of a portal thrown open to present a most inviting entrance between two close-hedges, soft and pouting. I could not but wish, observing this twin display of female charms, that I was myself among the company of ruffians, straining at the ropes with many a ribald remark and many an oath.

The umpire now gave the order to begin, and his two stewards let out the first of the recruits that stood at the head of the jostling, ardent line. This ruffian hesitated a moment and then went to enrol himself in the arms and army of the fair one; at which the company sent up a cheer, much to the annoyance of the umpire who must call us all to order. I know not whether it was because of the greater perfection of one of the smoothest, roundest, whitest bellies on which I ever have feasted my gaze or because no soldier wishes to be the first to make a breach in a redoubt, but the next recruit and the one after him make straight for the fair one. By this time, the dark one is looking extremely vexed; but she spreads her thighs yet wider, in even more insistent invitation, displaying something of which nothing in nature could be of a lovelier cut, the dark umbrage of the downy spring-moss that over-arched it bestowing on the luxury of that landscape a touching warmth, a tender finishing beyond the expression of words or even the paint of thought. At once one brawny rascal makes for her at the run and then another and another enlists under the same banner. The sun by now was going up the sky; and soon overheated and exhausted by their exertions, the two ladies were calling on their seconds to furnish them with eau de vie. Neck and neck the two fillies ran, now one being revived with a sniff at the aromatic salts and now the other downing the re-creative sal volatile. The seconds busied themselves with the napkins; the louts in the enclosure became ever more rabid to join the colours. One lady near to me fainted clean away from the excitement and could only be revived by the burning, beneath her nostrils, of her companion's peacock-feather fan. One elderly gentleman succumbed to a conniption and another all but succumbed to an apoplexy brought on by so unaccustomed a heating of the blood.

Now, as the ladies lay back in a contented near-swoon, from which they from time to time revived to cast baleful glances at each other, the umpire counted the numbers of the army beneath each banner. Then he recounted and counted yet again, to announce, to the consternation of all the company and the fury of the two contestants, that the numbers were exactly equal, forty-seven to forty-seven. At that Mr Swellington thrust forward: 'Let the casting vote lie in the hands – or between the legs – of this stalwart!' he called out. 'Let the choice lie with Mr Danny Hill!' At first the company all murmured in opposition to this proposal, saying that there was many a man of greater bottom to whom the privilege should more rightfully be accorded. 'Never mind the bottom!' cried out Mr Swellington. 'Feel the width!' By this time they had indeed looked at me more closely, though no one had laid hand on me, and all now concurred, including the ladies themselves, who clapped their hands in pleasure. But how was I to choose between two such delightful grottoes, each in perfect symmetry on either side of me? How happy I'd be in either, were t'other dear charmer away!

'Choose! Choose!' the company were now all bidding me; and the two ladies took up in an anguish of expectation: 'Yes, choose! Choose!'

I hesitated; I took one step towards the one and one step forward the other; I was well nigh unmanned by the mere excitement of the twin prospects before me. Then, my hand on my heart, I declared to the assembled people: 'Who can choose between the sky and the ocean, between the sun and the moon, between food and drink? I must needs have both and both must needs have me. Ladies –' I turned to them – 'may I be the mediator between the two of you, bringing reconciliation to you and both your armies.'

Without hesitation, both cried out, 'Yes! Yes!' at one and the same time. I held out a hand to each of them and drew them towards me. We had no need of couch, since the sward was soft enough; and when our sport was over, we had no need of restorative eau de vie or recreative sal volatile.

'Never more shall we quarrel, madam,' said the fair one.

'Never more,' sighed the dark one.

'That was indeed brave sport,' Mr Swellington said, when we had entered the carriage for our return. 'Was it not, John?'

But John remained sunken in a state of splenetic melancholy, saying nothing and not even raising his head.

Then Mr Swellington began to chide him: 'Forsooth, must you be so woebegone because of so superficial a wound in love's battles? The soldier knows well that he is as like to spill his gore as gain himself some glory. The sailor may as like sink to the bottom of the sea as raise himself to the heights of honour. Even the merchant who sets off for the Indies may find for himself not the expected fortune but an unexpected fever. You should be thankful that, unlike Guido, you have not lost something irrecoverable.'

'My Hetty is irrecoverable; or, rather, the idea that once I had of her,' replied John in great despondency.

'And good riddance,' said Mr Swellington, 'to her, as to all illusions!'

'What can be a greater illusion than yourself?' John demanded with unwonted asperity.

'I want no impertinence – from you, or from any man, or from any woman for that matter!'

John sank yet more deeply into a slough of despond; Harriet began to babble on about some young spark who, in the press, had managed to ignite her; and I, closing my eyes, fell asleep to dream of my beloved Lucy.

5

As one day succeeded another, so the initial excitement that I had derived from each performance of my duties, however arduous or protracted, began, perhaps inevitably, to evaporate. What I now felt, rather, was a satisfaction akin to that experienced by Harriet as he plied his needle at a tapestry cover for one of Mr Swellington's chairs, the aristocratic delicacy of his work in diverting contrast to the rustic coarseness of his subject matter (two cocks at contest, the pit waiting to receive them). The only difference was that, whereas *petit point* was his speciality, *gros point* was mine. Often I would have occasion to reflect on one of the saddest facts of human existence: namely, that repetition will soon make a routine out of even the wildest raptures. But I would then comfort myself with the reflection that, even as Mr Swellington had promised Harriet a goodly reward just as soon as his handiwork was ready, so too he was retaining on my account a perpetually growing sum of monies that might at last enable me to be reunited with my beloved Lucy. Once or twice I was tempted to ask him for the wherewithal to resort to the play or to Vauxhall, to buy myself this or that knick-knack or gewgaw or to betake me to the tables; but he would then answer me, 'Do not fritter away your substance but let me keep it under lock and key for you. The day may come when that other substance will dry at its source and you will be as glad of your thrift with the one as you will regret your prodigality with the other.' Heeding such advice, I would congratulate myself on having found such a good, loyal and kindly employer and friend.

One forenoon Mr Swellington summoned me to his chamber in a high good humour and, having popped into my mouth a comfit that I ill desired at such a time but that I accepted for fear of causing him offence, he informed me that shortly a gentlewoman would be arriving with the purpose of looking me over, before employing me. I did not greatly care for this 'looking over' since by then my reputation had been bruited abroad and such wine as I had to furnish to slake the thirst of my customers no longer needed any bushel. But Mr Swellington explained that, though not of the aristocracy, this was a lady whose husband had made a vast fortune in trade, purveying soap and similar commodities to every quarter of the civilized globe; that she herself had some distinction as a writer, albeit not as great as she believed to be due to her; and that she wished to procure my services, not for a single soirée or matinée but for a long period. Her name was Mrs Beak.

'But surely,' I asked, 'if I am to spend so much time with her, her husband will grow suspicious and jealous?'

'La, no!' Mr Swellington reassured me, attempting to push another comfit between my lips. 'He is the most complaisant creature in the world. Whatever she does, no matter how ridiculous or reprehensible, is a source of constant pleasure to him.'

'Perhaps he resorts to some secret diversions of his own?' I hazarded.

'Not unless the perusing of ledgers and the concoctions of receipts for his saponaceous products may be regarded as diversions. He is a very good, kind, *ordinary* gentleman, so I have heard tell. But Mrs Beak but rarely receives him in her drawing-room and I doubt if she has received him in her bed for many a long day. The company she prefers is all poetasters, penny philosophers, pedants, bluestockings, and every other pest and parasite of the whole scribbling race.'

At this a coach could be heard approaching over the

cobbles, with Tray, the mongrel bitch that the cook kept by her in the kitchen, setting up a wild latration.

'Here she comes! Withdraw a moment, Danny; but do not go further than the closet, so that you may hear all that passes. When I have occasion to summon you, then make your way out of the other door of the closet and come round to us. Hasten!'

Putting my eye to a crack in the door of the closet, I was somewhat disappointed to observe a short and squab body, somewhat over middle-age, with a large chin and a nose equally large and black eyes that, under bushy eyebrows, seemed like a pair of tiny currants. 'Lawks!' she exclaimed, breathing heavily, her face all glistening and a hand to her panting bosom. 'You have a great number of stairs, madam!'

'I hardly notice them,' said Mr Swellington. 'But pray be seated. Harriet will bring you a restorative beverage.'

Mrs Beak protested but Mr Swellington would hear nothing of it. 'The beverage is made according to a secret receipt that I had from an old country-woman. It is miraculously efficacious for all conditions.'

Harriet brought the glass but the old dame seemed reluctant to drink from it, taking but a simple sip and then putting it down, despite Mr Swellington's urgings that no cow's teat had ever yielded up a milk so rich and recreative to all the faculties of man or woman.

'To business, if it please you!' said Mrs Beak, smoothing her skirt with plump hands that, I could not fail to notice, were all a-glitter with a superabundance of rings. 'You have a young man in mind for me?'

'The most outstanding that the heart could desire!'

'I trust that his qualities are immediately apparent to the eye?'

'Absolutely, madam.'

'He is such a one that I may, without fear or prejudice, introduce to my friends?'

'That depends on the extent to which you can trust to their honour. I should not wish a jewel to be filched from you. I make bold to say that he is one of even greater worth than any that glitters on your fingers.' Mrs Beak gave a deep, contented sigh and my patron continued: 'He is the nicest, most prudent, best-conned young man that you could ever imagine. When I say that he can talk like a book, I do not mean one of those French novels now in vogue but such a book of the sort that you yourself have written for the delectation and instruction of the lettered world.'

'I hope that he is not *too* sober and sombre.'

'Indeed no, madam – no more than those effusions of your genius. But he is a very proper, well-behaved young man.'

'I should not wish him to be so well behaved that none of the company would notice him.'

'No one can fail to notice my Danny, just as no one could fail to notice Mr Punch.'

'He is ugly then?'

'I was not referring to his nose, madam.'

Mrs Beak seemed well satisfied. 'Good, good,' she said, smoothing down her skirts yet again and then venturing to take another sip from the beverage. 'Indeed, this cordial has a certain curious savour to it. It reminds me of something but I know not what. Many years have passed since I tasted anything similar.' She now drank readily from the glass and then set it down again. 'Might I glimpse this paragon?'

'Certainly, madam. I have told him to wait in readiness. I shall ring for him.'

But Mrs Beak stayed Mr Swellington before he could do so, declaring that there was one thing that she must needs ascertain before proceeding any further. Was Lady Gloria Garvice perhaps a patron of the house?

I had heard tell of this purveyor of just such 'French' novels as those to which Mr Swellington had recently alluded but I had myself never set eyes on her.

'Lady Gloria Garvice! Lord no, madam!' Mr Swellington exclaimed, agitating his fan like some frenzied peacock.

84

'To pose such a question suggests that you are ill acquainted with the nature and usages of this house. This house is one in which decorum is *de rigueur*. I could hardly hope to retain the custom of my clientele, much less the services of such as Danny, if I were to lower the tone by admitting such as Lady Gloria Garvice.'

'Hers is one of the oldest family-trees in the country.'

'That may indeed be so. But the oldest trees are often the most rotten.'

'And Lady Gloria Garvice has never clapped eyes on this Danny of yours?'

'I should sincerely hope not! As I have told you, madam, Danny is a most proper, well-behaved gentleman.'

'Good! You have fully relieved me. You may ring now, Mrs Swellington.'

When I came into the room, the old dame circled me as though I were some inanimate object in a gallanty-show with many an exclamation of wonder and pleasure. 'He has a nice cut of leg,' she said; and then, 'Yes, I find his *taille* wholly excellent.'

'Then I shall send him to you? I presume, madam, that you do not wish to consume the repast on the premises?'

'Perhaps I could take him with me now?'

'*Now*?'

'Since my carriage is below.'

Mr Swellington looked at me, to judge my wishes before making answer. 'I have no objection to going with Mrs Beak now, if she so wills it.'

'I have a dinner for some friends and I should wish the gentleman to be present.' Mrs Beak explained.

'You realize, of course, madam, that if the young gentleman is served up as a *bonne bouche* to all and sundry at the dinner, then some financial . . .'

'That was not my intention,' Mrs Beak responded stiffly. 'The young gentleman will be reserved exclusively for my own delectation.'

'If Danny would like to leave the room and wait outside, I can acquaint you with our tariff, madam.'

85

'The cost is immaterial!'

At this, I felt that, despite her unpleasing appearance, Mrs Beak had much to recommend her; a view in which Mr Swellington evidently concurred, since he beamed as he said, 'As you wish, madam! As you wish! Then you will trust me to send in my account in due course?'

'Perfectly.' Mrs Beak then went on to say that My Lady This and Her Grace That had been fulsome in their praise of Mr Swellington, for whose discretion and care for their interests they had the highest regard. It was only subsequently that I discovered that Mrs Beak rarely, if ever, mingled with people of such quality.

In her carriage, Mrs Beak simpered at me and then said: 'I trust that we shall be friends, Danny.'

'I trust so too, madam.'

'You seem to me to be ideally fitted for my purpose.'

'I am glad to hear it.'

I did not then realize what that purpose was to be, supposing it to be just such a purpose as that of any other of the women to whose wants I had heretofore attended. Mrs Beak continued:

'Are you acquainted with my works?'

I deliberated briefly whether to tell a falsehood or not, but then, deciding that perhaps the good woman might catch me out in any deviation from the truth, I confessed: 'Alas, madam, such has never been my good fortune. My wits, I fear, would be too shallow for your profundities.'

'That would appear to be the general opinion,' Mrs Beak remarked with evident bitterness. 'I am often praised and seldom read. But you are acquainted with the works of Lady Gloria Garvice?'

'In an idle moment I did indeed pick up a volume by that author. What I read had something to do with the attempted ravishment of a nun, if I remember rightly. But her work seemed to me both offensive and jejune and I did not proceed with it.' (In actual fact, Harriet had many of Lady Gloria's opera, which I would borrow off him and read with an avidity of which I cannot but be ashamed. I should have confessed this to my new employer had I not guessed that it would lower me vastly in her esteem.)

'Though so high-born, the woman is in truth nothing but a common trull. You have seen her name in the scandal-sheets?'

'The scandal-sheets, madam? I know nothing of scandal-sheets.' (Once again, I forbore to confess that Mr Swellington would enliven many of our moments of solitariness by reading out to us some information or other about the amatory exploits of this Lady Gloria.)

'What an innocence this is! You must not confess to such innocence before my friends. Else they will suppose that your behaviour is as innocent as your understanding.' Mrs Beak tapped my arm with her fan as she thus admonished me. Then she went on: 'The name of Lady Gloria is in every scandal-sheet. In the pot-houses they sing ribald ballads about her. She has been the occasion of many a lampoon, skit, squib and pasquinade. She is the talk of the whole town, of the whole country, indeed of the continent! You must have heard talk of her, Danny?'

'I have indeed heard something, madam.'

'And have you ever heard anything of *me*?'

'Of you, madam?'

'Of course you have not! I am, it is generally acknowledged among the cognoscenti, a writer of far greater worth than that wretched woman. Yet apart from the cognoscenti, who has heard of me, who ever reads me? Ours is a world, Danny, in which the only fame is ill fame; in which to gain a reputation, it is necessary for a woman to lose her reputation. Because I am a virtuous wife and a tender mother, because my works are such as would not bring a blush to the most modest of cheeks, in the eyes of the world I am nothing! I have published not less than forty-seven pious and improving volumes; I am quoted from pulpits up and down the land; His Majesty himself could find nothing reprehensible in my *Night Thoughts*, indeed complimented me on them. But my fame is as a brief shower to a tempest when compared with that hussy's.'

Mrs Beak was by now distressing herself so considerably, her face growing crimson, that I was relieved when the carriage turned into the courtyard of a splendid mansion hard by Piccadilly. Two menservants ran out to help us alight, one informing his mistress that the master had sent to enquire whether he was expected at the table that night; to which Mrs Beak replied that the company was such that it were better if he did not make an appearance.

'Come, dear Danny,' she said, sidling against me and offering me her arm, with a brazenness that amazed me in front of the servants. Then together we mounted the most splendid double stairway that ever you did see, she puffing asthmatically and hanging heavily from me, so that I had the impression that I was dragging a sack of coals up beside me.

'You will wish to prepare yourself for my guests,' she told me in the vestibule. Behind us, the two menservants were carrying up my trunk with many a gasp and groan, but it could hardly have weighed as heavy as their mistress. 'If there is anything of which you have need, please be sure to give your order for it. Your chamber has been prepared for you. It connects with my own.'

I was delighted with my lodgement, everything being of the utmost luxury and the windows looking out on to an extensive garden. One of the two menservants came in to ask if I required anything and then, gawping down impertinently at me, asked if I were from Mrs Swellington's. I replied haughtily that that indeed was my provenance, at which he muttered something about, ' 'Tis mighty strange,' as he prepared to leave the room.

'Stay!' I called after him. 'What is so mighty strange?'

An ill-favoured fellow, with reddish hair and eyebrows and the narrowest waist you ever saw on a man, he smirked and said: ' 'Tis unlike my lady to frequent Mrs Swellington's, she being so pious and precise. I cannot imagine her taking pleasure in aught that your mistress has to offer – or indeed, that you have to offer, good sir. Mayhap she is intent on regeneration.'

'Regeneration?'

'You have not read my mistress's tract on the Saving of Souls?' I shook my head. 'She is one,' the fellow went on, 'who believes that even the most hardened sinner may be redeemed.'

Even more haughtily than ever, I bid him to be gone. But I was perturbed at the thought that possibly this Fisher for Souls was attempting to fish for mine.

The most ridiculous company assembled, all chattering like a cageful of Barbary apes and not a one listening to his fellow. A languid young man, having quizzed me through his glass for several seconds, came over and introduced himself to me in an affected drawl. 'No doubt you have heard of me?' he demanded. When I replied that alas, I had not had that good fortune, he tossed his head like any pettish miss and said, 'But indeed, sir, you must have read or at least heard of my latest volume.' When again I was obliged to reply that alas, I had not had that good fortune, he replied that it was *vastly amusing* that I should be ignorant both of a poet of his eminence and a work that was the talk of all literary London. What was the subject? I ventured; to which, enunciating with undue care as though to a hottentot, he replied that the work was entitled *Ranae Historia Naturalis* – a natural history of the frog in heroic couplets. At that, he turned from me with an exclamation of impatience, to cry out, 'My Lady Frowsty by all that's wonderful!' as he hurried over to an ancient beldame as dishevelled and wild as any gypsy.

Mrs Beak now took my arm and, with many endearments, introduced me to the rest of the company, saying, 'This is my beloved Mr Danny Hill,' 'Here is the Apollo who has shed his light into my darkness,' 'Do you not agree that Mr Hill is the prettiest gentlemen in all the world?' and other such nonsense that filled me with embarrassment, being spoken to such a grave company of people, whom I had never set eyes on before. At table her conduct was even more scandalous, for while there was a discussion in train about the Good, the True and the Beautiful, what must she do but chuck me under the chin, pinch my cheek and pat my knee, drawing her chair so close to mine that I could hardly raise the food to my mouth without striking my elbow against the prominent overmantle of her bosom. But the company were so taken up with their argument that, mercifully, they seemed hardly to notice us. All at once, she told me: 'Now, come, Danny! Paddle a little in my bosom!'

'*Now*, madam?'

'Yes, now. 'Tis said that there is no time like the present.'

'But, madam, in such a reverent company. . . .'

'Do as I bid, Danny!'

So I needs must do as I am bid, clandestinely dipping my fingers in the finger-bowl when I have done, since the good lady was far from clean. But yet again no one in the company remarked anything amiss.

After we had eaten of a meal so frugal and plain that I marvelled at it, Mrs Beak announced that Signora Francolini would entertain us at the harpsichord. She arranged herself on the sofa and then bid me sit beside her, adding, 'I cannot bear that my beauteous Danny should absent himself from me even for a moment. Come, sir!' At that she took my hand in hers and, most immodestly, held it to her flaming cheek.

Signora Francolini raised a caterwauling even shriller and more unharmonious than Guido's; and all the time Mrs Beak must needs fondle and pet me, even feeling my riding-muscle with such indiscretion that I must beg her to forbear. 'Demonstrate your feelings for me, Danny! Let there be nothing secret between us! Give me your lips, I hunger for your lips!'

'Later, madam, later!' I hissed, aware that La Francolini was now embarked on some sacred cantata.

'But why, Danny, why?' she countered, throwing herself upon me.

'Such behaviour ill becomes you, madam,' I said, terrified lest the whole company might be observing what was happening. But some were listening or were pretending to listen to the music; some were still arguing among themselves in barely lowered voices; my poet was reading his own book, with obvious satisfaction; and some were asleep.

'Sure, 'tis a magnificent riding-muscle. You must have mastered many a jade in your day.'

'A few, madam, a few,' I said, attempting to wriggle away from her.

Such an evening I had never expected to pass in a house that I had supposed to be dedicated to the Muses, not to Priapus. If I attempted to retreat, the lady pursued; if I attempted to disengagement, she was hot on me. There was not a sofa or chair, not a crook or cranny into which I did not withdraw and into which she did not follow, with her cries, of 'Danny! Danny!' and, 'Why must you play me such tricks?' It seemed to me wondrous strange that, with such a reputation for rectitude, she should now be prepared to hazard all on a single, immediate toss.

'Wait, madam! Wait!' I begged her. 'We do not wish to be the scandal of London! And what will Mr Beak say? Even the servants are watching.' But still she pursued me with insistent lips and fingers.

After what seemed to me to be an eternity, the company finally took their leave; and then, most strangely, Mrs Beak at once became as cold to me as previously she had been fiery. 'Then I shall bid you goodnight, Mr Hill. On the morrow we shall drive in Hyde Park, when I hope you will be more showing to me.' At that she turned and mounted the stairs, in seeming dudgeon.

At first, I was relieved at my escape; but then, bethinking me of all that wealth that Mr Beak had amassed from the sale of his saponaceous products and feeling also, it must be confessed, a certain stiffness and ache in my riding-muscle after all that squeezing and pulling, I resolved to go in unto the lady, who was obviously in such a state of excitation that otherwise she might not sleep. I therefore first divested myself of all but my most intimate garments, slipped into a robe of the most rare Chinese silk that had been set out for me and knocked on the door between her chamber and mine. There being no answering voice, I knocked again, yet more loudly. Then I heard a most pitifully affrighted: 'Yes? Who is it? Who is it?' But how could the lady not know that it was I, since it was she who had given orders for me to be lodged in the chamber hard by hers?

'It is I, Danny Hill,' I gave answer.

'What do you want? It is late and I must needs be up betimes to go to St Martin's.'

This seemed to me wondrous strange; but already at Mr Swellington's I had met women in whom the desire to be conquered was so strong that they would dissimulate their passion with many a show of false modesty, prudery and perturbation. Assuming her to be playing just such a game, I cried out with all the ardour that I could muster (in truth, it was not much): 'I needs must see you. I cannot be denied. You have lit such a fire within me this night that only you can quench it.'

'To bed, Danny! Enough!' And at that, I heard her approach the door and turn the key in the wards.

Still willing enough to play out her pantomine with her, I bellowed out in the voice of one in the extremes of anguish: 'Madam! Madam! Mercy! Have mercy! I burn! I faint! I fail!' hammering the while on the door that lay between us.

Again the key turned in the wards and Mrs Beak pulled open the door, barely recognizable now that her wig was removed to reveal on her head as much down as you will see on a day-old chick and her body all a ruinous slide and tumble downwards now that her stays had been unlaced. 'What is the meaning of this, sirrah? How dare you disturb my incipient repose in such an unmannerly fashion?'

By now this drama was growing mighty tedious to me

but, feeling that I needs must play along a little more, I threw myself upon her. 'How may I melt this snow? Must I freeze to death like one cast out to die on some mountain peak? Madam! Madam!'

She gave out a fearful ululation and then fastened her teeth, which were fortunately neither many nor sharp, in the arm that I had placed about her. 'Unhand me, sir! Else I shall summon the servants and have you returned to your mistress forthwith.'

There was such in her tone and demeanour that at last made it clear to me that she was by no means other in than in earnest.

'But, madam,' I stammered, 'I can in no way comprehend you. Throughout this evening you have fanned the flames, so overtly that I feared for a scandal concerning our names. Now you wish to throw a bucket of water on the conflagration that you yourself have provoked. I know not what to make of all this; my wits are addled; I float at random in a sea of perplexity. Having given me so many assurances, can you now deny me?'

'Danny, I am a woman of propriety and religion. That for many a long year I have been too much taken up with redeeming the heathen, defending the faith and writing the tracts, pamphlets, homilies, discourses, pandects, treatises, dissertations, sermons and such like on which my future fame will rest, to accommodate the admittedly less and less insistent demands of Mr Beak, does not mean that I am therefore desirous of accommodating those of someone unknown to me until this afternoon. . . .'

'But, madam, I am all at a loss,' I stammered, as indeed I was. 'Can I have misunderstood all those seemingly obvious demonstrations of your high regard for me? Did your hand not seek out mine? Did your lips not search out my lips? Did you not pour sugared nothings into the conch of my ear? Did you not, indeed, attempt to assess the strength of my riding-muscle?'

At that, she opened the door wide and, with an indication of that bald head of hers, invited me to enter. 'Pray be seated, Danny. But do not defile my marital bed and do not approach too near to me, seeing that I am now all in dishabille. I realize that I needs must tell you all, for fear that you will enter into an even greater state of perplexity before I have done with you. But you must promise me your utmost discretion and silence in this matter.'

'You may trust to me, madam. I already have many professional secrets locked up in my bosom, that I should as soon violate as a physician would violate his Hippocratic oath.'

'Good. Then to begin! You have heard me complain already of the fame of Lady Gloria Garvice – of how even the most ignorant apprentice knows of her and her iniquities; of how you may not attend any rout or ball or party without hearing constant mention of her name; of how you may not open any scandal-sheet, whether English or foreign, without seeing her doings inscribed in it. Yet it is generally acknowledged that, whereas I am one of the glories on the face of our literature, she is but a pock, papula or pustule. 'Tis foolish, I know, to be envious of such a slut and yet, I know not why, virtuous, charitable and decent woman that I am, that woman has nonetheless ignited in my breast a flame of envy as fiery as that flame of lust that I but recently have ignited in yours. I must emulate her; I must win the selfsame reputation, however malodorous; I must achieve the selfsame fame, however frail. Thus, though the majority of my sisters wish to be secret votaries of vice and public proponents of virtue, in my case it is just the reverse. I wish all the world to think that I am so besotted with you that I can no longer rein in the steed of my passion and, Mazeppa-like, must hurtle to my self-destruction; I wish to become the common talk of the coffee-houses, pot-houses, kips, bagnios, bawdy-houses and stews; I wish to be caricatured, lampooned, satirized, aspersed and aviled – none of this being of any moment to me, providing only that I am known and talked about throughout the length and breadth of this country and even across the seas. But, at the same time, that I should retain for the use of my husband or, to be more accurate, for no use at all, the jewel priceless above all diamonds and rubies is no more than I owe to Mr Beak, to myself and, above all, to Him who made it and me along with it.'

'You stupefy me, madam!'

'It is difficult, perhaps, to appreciate the nicety of one such as I.'

'Indeed.'

'You seemed to be the best instrument of my plan. One so young; so ardent; so provoking to the eye and so pleasing to the touch: those who saw you with me must needs believe that I should not set my knife and fork to such a dish unless I were planning to eat it. But in your occupation as my *cavaliere servente*, it will be your duty to serve only by standing and waiting. In public I wish you to lavish every possible proof of the ardour of your affections, so that the fact cannot but catch the eye of even the most negligent observer; I, in turn, will act the part of Lady Gloria in the throes of one of her brief and blatant infatuations. But in private, I must ask you to treat me with the same reserve, politeness and decorum that you would show to your own mother.'

'Alas, I do not know who or where my mother is or how I should behave to her, if we were to be reunited.'

Mrs Beak was not interested in hearing of either my mother or my misfortunes and was now about to dismiss me, rising from her chair and holding the door to my chamber open for me in peremptory manner.

'It will be difficult for me to find repose, madam,' I said. 'I am now in such a state of excitation that I am sore tempted to seek out that Lady Gloria Garvice herself.'

'Marry come up!' I had spoken but in jest but Mrs Beak had taken me in earnest and was now angered with me. 'I forbid any such thing. I shall summon Maria to bring you my grandmother's warming pan.' At that she went and pulled at the bell. 'Maria is but a heathen girl, brought back from the Africk shores, whom I should wish to convert, were she possessed of any understanding. But the customs of her country have made her impervious to sound sense and decent doctrine. When she was found by an English sea-captain of my acquaintance on some desolate, tropic strand, she was in a state of nature and sustaining herself on molluscs and kelp. She has now taken to dressing herself in a manner that would be more becoming to a lady than to one of her humble station (do not ask me how she comes by the wherewithal) and to eating only the most delicate of foods. But all my efforts to make her clothe herself in righteousness and swallow the doctrines of the Church have, alas, proved in vain. The poor misguided Hottentot takes more thought for her Sunday bonnet than for Sunday observance and infinitely prefers some succulent casserole of meats to the Catechism.'

'But I have no need of a bedpan, madam. It is quite another kind of receptacle of which I am desirous.'

' 'Tis only a figure of speech. We are a very nice household and in no nice household is a spade called anything other than an implement of excavation. My grandmother was a lady of the bedchamber to the Merry Monarch and when, being inordinately Merry, he desired a particular service of her, he would summon her to fetch him the bedpan. . . . Ah, here is the wench!'

Maria was black as Egypt's night, with the most lustrous ebony skin on which I had ever gazed and two globes that might well have done service in a game of bowls. Her teeth were as pearls and the whites of her eyes vied with them for candour. As she dropped me a curtsey, she gave me at the same time a marvellously roguish look, as though she had already divined the purpose for which she had been summoned. The happy valley was deep and bedewed with pearls of moisture – the fond wench was evidently already overheated, whether from running up the stairs or at the prospect before her I cannot say.

'Maria, this gentleman, Mr Danny Hill, requires a service of you.'

Before Mrs Beak could expound further, the little minx takes up: 'De bedpan, and please my lady?'

'Precisely. Go get it ready. See that it is thoroughly scoured so that such a nice gentleman may pick up no contamination from it and sprinkle a little rosewater over it.'

'Yes, ma'am.'

Maria scuttled from the room in evident delight.

'I should not allow any decent gel of those that serve me to be used in such a manner, for fear that she might hazard her immortal soul. But since the poor heathen recks not a tittle for that soul of hers, if indeed she is possessed of one, it is of no account. She will go to perdition one way or another, for all my preaching and pleading.'

Shortly after the little Hottentot came in to me, all a-twitter and a-titter. Used as I was to ladies intent to persuade me that they yielded to my importunities only perforce, I was surprised to meet now with one of the fairer sex (if indeed I may call fair one who was so wondrously dark) who was totally without any modesty or coyness. In no time at all, she lay motionless, breathless, dying with dear delight beneath me, her eyes revealing, through their nearly closed lids, just the edges of their black, the rest being rolled vehemently upwards in their ecstasy, her tongue leaning, negligently crimson, towards the lower range of her pearly teeth, and the natural ruby of her full lips glowing with heightened life. Her only disappointment (such as no damsel had ever experienced before) was with my riding-muscle, which she declared outstripped any other that she had seen in this country but was, nonetheless, inferior to those to be found in her own heathen land.

When compressed, squeezed and distilled to the last drop, I was about to take my leave of her, she would have none of it, but, 'More, more, more!' was all her cry. Now she was all on top of me in a tangle of hair and limbs; then, like some marmoset from her place of origin, the minx was swinging from the chandelier with such abandon that I feared as much for Mrs Beak's Waterford glass as for her repose in the next-door chamber. At last, I contrived to restrain her, with many a promise of sweets in store for the morrow and a liberal bounty from my purse. She kissed the coins in my palm, saying, 'Love, love, love' (whether in reference to me or the money I know not) and then, pleadingly, 'More, more, more!' with increasing shrillness and urgency until Mrs Beak could be heard from the next-door chamber, saying in peremptory fashion, that would not be denied: 'Have done, Maria! Remove the bed-pan instanter and see that it is well emptied and washed out!'

At that the little minx, who evidently held her mistress in greater awe than she held me, scuttled from the room and I was able to fall on my bed in a condition of satiety and exhaustion such as I had never experienced before in my life. Before Morpheus sealed my eyes, I remember thinking: 'Another such motion like that and I shall be beyond the art of the most cunning apothecary or physician.'

On the morrow, Mrs Beak took me, as she had forewarned, in her coach to Hyde Park, sitting so close to me that I could hardly draw breath and all the time fondling and petting me as impudently as on the night before. But again no one paid us any heed. At one point in our progress, she cried out, pointing with her fan: 'There she is! The brazen madam! But take a look at her!' Everyone else in the Park was also taking a look, the coachmen negligent of their horses, the poorer sort negligent of their perambulators and the babies in them, the men of fashion quizzing, the women of quality gawping. It was only the briefest of visions; but never, except for my Lucy, had I set eyes before on such a paragon of beauty, her skin as transcendently fair as Maria's had been transcendently dark, the whiteness of her arms such as to put the lily out of countenance and, above all, her looks so candid and sweet that I could not believe that here indeed was that Messalina of whom I had heard and read so much. Beside her was a gallant, whom Mrs Beak later told me was some kind of scribbler of the baser sort; but I hardly noticed him, any more than one notices a star that is contiguous to the full moon.

'Observe, observe!' cried Mrs Beak in a frenzy of passion. 'She has but to sit there, as cool as any cowcumber, barely acknowledging him who is her paramour, and all London must needs stare and all the news-sheets must needs write about her. But here am I, so close to a Ganymede, and none pays any heed at all! 'Tis most provoking!'

It was the same at the play that evening, with many a savant, blue-stocking, preacher and prelate coming and going in my lady's box, and none paying the smallest heed as she must most shamelessly dally, buss, coquet, cast sheep's eye, toy, fondle, cocker and who knows what besides and I must, at her bidding, reciprocate. One might have thought that such conduct would have either emptied or filled the theatre; that Mr Garrick would have been at a loss to proceed with Hamlet's soliloquies; that we should have been execrated, anathematized and even lapidated. But our behaviour might have been above all reproach for all the notice that we occasioned. Meanwhile, in the box opposite, there was Lady Gloria Garvice, surrounded by gallants, her shoulders and swelling breasts glimmering and her hair a golden torrent. She paid no attention to anyone but Mr Garrick; and everyone, including Mr Garrick, paid attention only to her.

On subsequent days we strolled by the Thames; attended balls and routs; took a cup of coffee at My Lady This and a dish of tea at My Lady That; attended morning service at St Martin's and evening service at St Matthew's; went to buy a new bonnet for my mistress and a new jacket for myself. Mrs Beak was no less shamelessly importunate than heretofore, indeed was even more so; and though wearied by my nightly use of the bedpan,

I must needs in turn comply with her instructions as best I might. But yet again we might have been airy phantasms for all the notice we provoked.

At last, after a long and wearisome week, Mrs Beak summoned me to her bedchamber. 'Danny,' she declared, 'it is all to no avail. It will not do.'

'I hope that I have not fallen short, madam. No lady has ever had occasion to say that of me.'

'You have given me every satisfaction – or, at least, every satisfaction that I have required of you – and I shall tell your mistress accordingly. Indeed, if you so wish it, I shall put it into writing, for a reference from me, whether for a book, for a sermon or for such labour as yours, must carry weight in the world. But I see that my plan, seemingly so secure, was built on a foundation of ignorance. It grieves me to confess as much; for I am generally regarded as one the of least ignorant, indeed as one of the most erudite, of my sex. But I have spent so much of my time in my study of what is written that I have omitted to observe what is done.

'We are all what the world believes us to be. Having formed its opinion of us, it will not be disabused. Lady Gloria Garvice, even though she were to lead a life of blameless domesticity such as my own, would nonetheless, in popular credence, be regarded as a Messalina. Even were I to resort to all the excesses of Messalina herself, I should nonetheless continue to be regarded as a Cornelia. It is difficult enough to change what we are; it is even more difficult to change what the world thinks that we are. A writer may, having appeared as a noodle in his first works, later compose poetry worthy of a Milton or a Shakespeare; to the world at large he will not be a Milton or a Shakespeare but still a noodle. Or he may start out with the tongue of an angel and then decline into the neighing of a donkey; to the world at large he will still be an angel and no one will see his long ears. Even were you to ravish me in full view of His Majesty and all St James's, no one would think any ill of me. I have written too many tracts, rescued too many souls, lived too long a life of the utmost propriety. I must abandon the struggle. I am sorry, Danny.'

'I, too, am sorry, madam,' I answered, though I was far from being so, since I was eager to be rid of the embarrasment of seeming to pay court to someone so frumpish and ill-favoured.

'Tell your mistress that I shall call tomorrow to settle my account.'

'I can take the money with me,' I volunteered.

'That is indeed kind of you, Danny. But Mrs Swellington was mighty insistent that accounts must be settled with her alone. Such, she told me, was her system.'

'As you and she wish. It is immaterial to me. But before I parcel up my chattels and betake myself away, might I perhaps crave a favour of you?'

'A favour? If it is the favour that I surmise is in your mind, I must repeat, dear Danny, that though you are the most obliging of gentleman, yet I am, as I have said, a woman of the utmost propriety and I cannot, alas, grant you anything that Mr Beak and my Maker would not wish me to grant.'

'All I wished, madam, was to use the bedpan once again before my departure.'

Mrs Beak looked mightily displeased at this request, drawing herself up to her full height (even though she still looked dumpy and dwarfish) and glaring at me with such a glance as I had so often witnessed her addressing at Lady Gloria. 'You can surely wait until you have reached Mrs Swellington's house!' she retorted.

I perceived that to argue further would be of no avail and retired to my chamber.

On my depature no servants hurried forward to carry my trunk down the stairs as once they had carried it up them; and there was no splendid equipage with coachman and outriders. I lifted my trunk on to my shoulder, heavy though it was, and having spent all my little store of coins on Maria, decided that I needs must walk. Then, on a sudden, I heard a calling of my name and, gazing all around me, I saw a black face peering out at me through the dusty window of a shed in one corner of the courtyard. 'Danny! Danny boy!'

I dropped the trunk and hurried in to her. What better place could be devised to use a bedpan than the jakes?

6

When at last, footsore and with aching loins and back, I once again reached Mr Swellington's establishment, it was to find everyone in a state of frenzied commotion, so that I guessed that either the law or company must be expected. But in both these surmises I was wide of the mark. Mr Swellington was no longer dressed out in his habitual furbelows and flounces but instead might have passed, in his pinafore, mob-cap and stout pair of boots, for some honest or not so honest fishwife in Billingsgate. Dashing up the stairs, he was calling out some order to the old woman for the preparation of hot water; at which she shouted back that the dratted boy had let the fire go out and could no wise be found.

Observing me, Mr Swellington exclaimed: 'Danny! So soon! Mrs Beak sent word but yesterday that she would retain you till the week's end.'

'Mrs Beak changed her mind.'

At that Mr Swellington, looking mightily alarmed, came back down the stairs to me: 'I trust you did nothing to displease her, Danny? Or is that you did not do sufficient to please her?'

'Neither. She told me that she was more than satisfied with such services as I could render. Indeed, she promised me a testimonial as to my standing.'

'Did she entrust any monies to you?'

'None. She will call tomorrow to settle her score.'

'Excellent.' It was immediately apparent that Mr Swellington was much relieved. Then he stared closely into my face: 'But Danny – why so peaked and pined? Did Mrs Beak not feed you properly?'

'Like herself, the fare was plain but ample.'

'Then how so?' I made no answer, not wishing my
patron to learn that, so far from having been paid recompense for my services to the witching Hottentot, it was
she who had repeatedly exacted recompense from me with
the same assiduity that she had exacted the balsamic fluid.
'Ah, who would have thought it of one such as Mrs Beak!'
Mr Swellington continued. 'So devout! So proper! Such
a one as thinks that her husband is taking a liberty if he so
much as tweaks her croupon and who would even bathe
in a shift for fear of looking on what no eye must observe
but the all-seeing eye of its Maker! 'Tis said that still
waters run deep; and in the same manner the glacier oft
conceals a geyser! What a sanctimonious strumpet! What
a pietistic punk! Who would believe it?'

I refrained from replying that it was precisely because
no one would believe it that I was now back so prematurely; and, instead, asked what was afoot.

'General Peabody's hour has come,' came the answer.
'And for fear of the scandal to his repute, he must needs
take asylum here with us. I enjoin you to the strictest
secrecy, for if rumour should reach the outside world that
the conqueror of half of India had been brought to bed
out of wedlock, he would be ruined, ruined utterly! You
may be present at the birth, Danny. Indeed, I am sure
that the good General would wish you to be so, along with
the father.'

I was totally perplexed by all this talk. 'The father?' I
queried, hoping thus to raise the enveloping veil a little.
'The General's father? I had thought that General Peabody was well advanced in years.'

'No, no, Danny! The father of his child – our Sammy!
Such a mesalliance the mind could not conceive! A high-
born gentleman and a mere tar! Wedlock in such circumstances is not conceivable.'

I had hardly supposed the General to be conceivable
either and, in my continuing bewilderment, would have
questioned Mr Swellington further if, at that very moment,

I had not heard a carriage clatter over the cobbles of the court without. 'Lawks!' shrilled Mr Swellington. 'He is come and Harriet is still laying clean linen to the bed and Martha is still heating up the water. And I, too, still have much to which I must attend. Go, Danny, and receive him.'

I went reluctantly out into the court; but there I could see no one who seemed to me in the smallest manner like the heroic general. Between them the coachman and a diminutive maidservant were helping down from the carriage a vast woman, all heavily veiled so that her visage was totally invisible, whose swollen belly proclaimed only too obviously that her time was nigh. She was emitting many a sigh and groan, clutching from time to time at that prominent belly of hers with a 'Lord have mercy!' or a 'Lord love-a-duck!' Now the maid and the coachman were supporting her towards me, her head far surmounting theirs, even though she was all but doubled over in the anguish of incipient labour. 'Easy, ma'am! Careful, ma'am! 'Twill soon be over! After a brief purgatory, there will be a long paradise!' So did the coachman and the maidservant attempt to hearten her; but at the words she let forth the most heartrending sobs, with: 'The paradise preceded the purgatory! Now I must needs pay for my complaisance! I yielded up my precious honour to that varlet and now I am dishonoured! Alack, I am ruined! An hour of pleasure must be paid with an eternity of shame! Obloquy, odium and opprobrium are now my lot!'

' 'Sh, madam! Have done! You will only harm the life nascent within you by such frenzies,' remonstrated the maidservant. Then she looked up, saw me, and emitted a little gasp.

'May I be of any assistance?' I asked. 'My name is Danny Hill and Mr – Mrs Swellington bade me to welcome you.'

'The poor lady is indeed very near her hour. Many was the time that I feared that we must needs halt the coach and the poor babe would be laid down in the fields or the gutter. The waters have broken,' she added, using a phrase that, such was my innocence, had no meaning for me.

'Is the midwife summoned?' the coachman asked.

'I know not. I have but lately returned home. But Mr – Mrs Swellington is putting all in readiness, of that I am assured.'

'Nine months ago I came here as a maid; now I shall leave here as a mother!' sobbed the poor creature, throwing herself about in the grasp of coachman and maidservant. 'Ichabod!'

Mr Swellington now hurried out. 'Ah, the poor lady, the poor lady!' and he, too, joined in supporting the sagging burden that I had been fearing might overstrain the little maidservant. ' 'Tis easy to see that her hour is at hand.'

'The waters have broken,' repeated the coachman.

'Lawks! You do not say so! Ah, the poor lady!'

Between us, the maid and coachman pulling and Mr Swellington and I pushing, we managed to get the lady into an upper bedchamber, where, abandoning all decorum, my patron and the maidservant began to strip her of her clothes. Imagine my amazement, when the veils had been removed, to see a coarse, weather-beaten visage with a copious grey moustache and beard. Like a thunderclap it burst on me; here was General Peabody! Hiding his face in the hands that had despatched many an infidel to his doom, he began to sob yet again: 'Ah, the shame of it, the dishonour, the humiliation! 'Tis the woman who pays – and pays – and pays yet again! The male kind have their will of us and reck not of what may follow after!'

' 'Tush, madam!' cried Mr Swellington, cradling the General, as best he might, in his arms and leading him to the bed, in nothing now but a shift. 'You will but harm yourself and the baby with such fretting and repining.'

'You are right, good midwife,' the poor wretch answered 'But how could I have been so blind to the example of my virtuous mother, taken from this world by our Maker in my infancy; to the teaching of my no less virtuous father; to all modesty and shame?'

He now suffered himself to be laid out on the bed, the old woman meanwhile bustling in with a steaming pail of water. 'A-a-a-a-h!' Never before had I heard a scream so piteous. 'The time is very near,' said Mr Swellington, rolling up his sleeves, to reveal such a brawny pair of arms that any midwife in the land would be proud to possess. 'Do you wish, madam, that your dear undoer be present?'

The General threw a hirsute arm across his brow. 'No, no! Keep hence that that loathsome Lothario, that Don Juan, that Bluebeard. Having engineered my shame, must the loose fish also witness it? Having laid the charge to the coffer, must that goat look on while it spills its contents?'

'As you wish, madam,' Mr Swellington said appeasingly. 'As you wish. . . . Now, if you would place your hands so – and your legs *so* – and bear down hard. . . .'

At that the poor wretch, though racked with pain, suffered a change of mind. 'After all, good midwife, you may summon him. Let him see how we frail women must pay in blood, sweat and tears for the concupiscence of the monstrous regiment of men. 'Tis I who will be called strumpet, trull, trollop, drab, bitch, slut and Cyprian the length and breadth of London. He will at most have the reputation of being a saucy gallant. Fetch him! Quick!'

Sam was now ushered into the room in his sailor's gear, very penitent, his cap being twiddled between his hands and his eyes downcast.

'Betrayer! Ravisher! Rake! See to what straits you have brought your innocent Evangeline!' the General cried out and then, writhing on the bed, he screamed with even more force than heretofore: 'A-a-a-a-ah!'

Mr Swellington, the old woman and the maidservant shook their heads; and then said simultaneously: 'The time is very nigh.'

'Bear down, my dear! Harder! Yet harder! The more the agony of it, the quicker 'twill be despatched.'

Suddenly, with a strangulated sob, Sam threw himself down beside the bed, kneeling as he held the large, hairy hand of the General to his lips. 'Forgive me, my angel, my cosset, my fondling! Had I but known, had I but thought, had I but seen –! He who steals a blackberry from a hedge recks not of the thorn that may, entering subtly, poison his whole body. Ah, my duck, my honey, my jewel!'

'I forgive you,' the General muttered. 'When the sap is rising in the blood; when a young man, overflowing with natural juices, sets eyes on one (modesty almost forbids me to say) of more than usual beauty, grace and charm; when the time, the place and loved ones are all together. . . . Yes, I forgive you, my jolly jack tar. How could I do otherwise? I forgive you my dear, dear, dearest destroyer.'

Through all this Sam was sobbing loudly over the hands he grasped.

Now the screams became even more frequent and even more piercing. Mr Swellington busied himself under the shift, the sweat starting from his forehead as profusely as from the General's, as he now encouraged or admonished him and now told us, gathered about the bed, that the head was already evident, that indeed the birth was imminent, that it would be but a short time before all was done. . . .

There was one final scream, like some damned soul in exquisite torment in the nether regions, and then from the General's own nether regions Mrs Swellington triumphantly plucked forth – a doll! At the sight, I was so much overcome by this pantomime of my own coming into the world that I all but swooned away.

There was much business of severing the navel-string, Harriet producing her pinking-shears for the purpose; and then much washing of the infant and much application of vinegar to the poor supine wretch's forehead and of spirits of ammonia to his nose (the moustache twitching mightily during this last business). The old woman produced a tumbler of *eau de vie*, which the General raised his head sufficiently to drain at a single gulp. I saw her pour herself a similar glass and drain it in the same fashion in a corner apart, no doubt overborne by all that we had witnessed.

Mr Swellington tossed the counterfeit babe in the air and then cuddled it against his breast. 'See what a beautiful chick it is!' he cried. 'A boy, a veritable boy! Oh, what a dainty dear!' Then he lowered the object towards the General: 'Good madam, take one look, for it must be your last. The baby-farmer is even now waiting below.'

At this the General took the doll to him, pressing it to his manly chest and showering it with kisses. Then in a tumult of sobbing, he handed it back to Mr Swellington: 'Adieu! A long adieu, an adieu as long as life is long! Bear him away!'

Mr Swellington bustled out, after first showing the doll to Sam, who took its tiny hand and bussed it. With many a sigh and groan, muttering from time to time, 'I am very weak, very weak,' the General rose from the bed and suffered the maidservant to dress him once again.

After a while first Guido and then John stole into the chamber. 'Madam,' said the one, 'a more beautiful child I have not yet seen in all my born days.'

'The foster-nurse is a good, decent woman,' said the other. 'Have no fears.' The General's only answer to all this was another fit of blubbing.

When he was once more swathed in veils, we supported him, sobbing and tottering, to his carriage. More than once the pert little maidservant gave me a glance and, as she peered out of the window of the carriage at the moment of departure, she even ventured a wink and a sign, with one hand, of which the meaning was obscure to me. We all then returned to the house, where Mr Swellington called for ratafee for all the company.

'The poor General,' he sighed, spreading himself on a sofa. 'Nine months since he was last in this house, he must needs make the perilous journey all the way back from India to be delivered.'

'I have never heard of such an aberration,' I remarked. ' 'Tis monstrous strange.'

'The General is often called the father of his troops. Perhaps it were better if he were called their mother.'

At that we all began to laugh most heartily and to congratulate each other on play-acting as good as any we had ever seen in the play-house, until Mr Swellington called a halt to our mirth: 'The poor wretch may, indeed seem risible to us. But it was the same capacity to dream and to make a reality of his dreaming that both brought him here to be delivered of a doll and took him to India to conquer half a continent.'

I could see that my patron and mentor was about to grow philosophical once again and hurriedly excused myself; as did also John, who followed me up the stairs to my room.

'How goes it, John?' I asked.

'For my body, all goes well. The burning flux has left me and Mr Swellington promises me that I may return to employment within a day or two. But my heart is like lead.'

'How so?'

' 'Tis true, since I myself proved it with so much pain, that my Hetty is nought but a cheating strumpet. But I have a desire for her company that no high-born lady – nor indeed any high-born gentleman – can vanquish within me. Her looks are no less lowly than her morals, her person no less filthy than her habits; but it is she and she only that I crave.'

'If that be so, 'tis best to forgive and forget and go to seek her out.'

'Such was my plan.' By now we had entered my chamber and with great care he shut the door upon us before he went on: 'But our mistress refuses to discharge me.'

'He cannot refuse.'

'She does so.'

'Then you needs only discharge yourself.'

'But she holds all my monies in trust on my behalf.'

'You must request them.'

'I have done so. But she says that they are all in the funds at six-and-one-half per cent and that it will take many a day to realize them for me. Without money, how shall I make my way in the world? And without money, how shall I make my way to Hetty's heart or to any other part of her.'

' 'Tis a quandary.'

'A quandary, indeed.'

After the disconsolate John had left me, I lay me down on the couch and thought over all that he had told me. If Mr Swellington made so much difficulty over rendering John his monies, might he not make the same or greater difficulties in my own case too? I had been hired as a servant. Could it be that, in reality, I had been indentured as a slave? In the world at large we see that every man from time to time becomes enslaved to passion. My enslavement had taken corporal form; and it was not an intermittent but a permanent state of being.

7

On the morrow Mrs Beak arrived betimes to pay her dues
to Mr Swellington, in the company of a woman as homely,
plump and plainly-dressed as herself. Seeing them, you
would have supposed them to be, not ladies of consequence and wealth, but two milliners on a Sunday
outing to church. There was much sniffing and frowning
and drawing up of dark-blue worsted skirts as the two
entered the house; but once having entered, they seemed
strangely reluctant to leave again. The other dame was
one Mrs Muggles, a member of some sect of Quakers or
such like, who abominated all drinking, gambling, play-
going, fornication and indeed every kind of pleasure other
than that of praising the Lord and making money. She
had, I later learned, a large brood of children, many of
whom were a source of constant expense, trouble and
shame to herself and her spouse; but such was her propriety that I can only suppose that they were conceived
by some process of parthenogenesis.

After Mrs Beak had handed over the money, Mr
Swellington, having noticed her unwillingness to make
her adieus, suggested that perhaps she and her companion
would care for a dish of tea. Mrs Muggles said, 'Indeed, I
do not know. . . ,' with a deep sigh, much as though she
had been asked to sup with the devil and had forgotten to
bring her long spoon with her. Mrs Beak then looked all
around her, as timorous as if she were alone on the highway on a night of no moon, and said: ' 'Tis wondrous hot
today. And I have such a thirst. . . . But I should not wish
to discommode you, good Mrs Swellington.'

'There is no discommodement. Harriet may leave her embroidery for a moment.'

'Such a pretty piece of work!' exclaimed Mrs Muggles, who was evidently short of sight. 'And such a pretty wench!'

'Pray seat yourself, ladies,' Mr Swellington urged.

Mrs Muggles did as she was bid and then turned to eye me. 'And so this is Mr Hill!' she said, much as one might say, 'And so this is a lion!'

'Yes, that is our Mr Hill, the pride and joy of this establishment.'

'By my troth, I could hardly credit it when good Mrs Beak informed me that such an establishment as this existed in the heart of our city. Were it in Paris or in the Lowlands, then my credulity would not have been strained to quite such a degree. I am only a simple, god-fearing woman and Mr Muggles is only a simple, god-fearing man. It seems to me wondrous strange that people should resort to you for the purchase of such a commodity.'

' 'Tis a commodity that will always be in demand,' Mr Swellington retorted. 'And the majority would prefer to be assured of buying goods that are not damaged and that are to be had at a fair price.'

'You provide a terrible snare for the world,' Mrs Muggles said, shaking her head, so that her jowls quivered, as she bent down to her dish of tea.

'On the contrary, madam, it is the world that provides a terrible snare for us. We should no doubt be going about some honest business or other, like good Mr Muggles, were it not that the world is so insistent that we should do something dishonest for its pleasure. We have not made the world as it is; the world has made us as we are.'

'You are very clever, Mrs Swellington, of that I am convinced. How may a poor, innocent woman such as myself argue with you?' She turned to Harriet: ' 'Tis an excellent brew you have made for us, my dear.' She sighed. 'So young that you are! And a prisoner in this house of ill fame!'

'Madam, I have no doubt that I live better here than any servant of yours,' Harriet retorted with warmth.

'Pert girl!' Mrs Muggles exclaimed.

Soon, Mrs Beak must once again begin to talk of her King Charles's Head, the glorious Lady Gloria. Such a hussy, such a whited sepulchre, such a tramp and trull! was all her theme. To this Mrs Muggles concurred, with many a sage nod, eventually taking up: ' 'Tis a disgrace that she should sully the purple into which she was born. *Noblesse oblige* does not signify that she must needs oblige every man who makes his demand of her.' She lent forward confidentially, setting down her dish of tea: 'An acquaintance of mine, a lady who moves more in the *beau monde* than Mrs Beak and I have either the opportunity or the desire to do, acquainted me of an interesting matter only yesterday. 'Twould seem that, when Lady Gloria is bent on dalliance, she first bids her prospective partner to dine with her at four o'clock or so. Whether the one appetite is sharpened by satisfying the other, I know not. But such, my acquaintance assured me, is her practice.'

'I have heard the same,' Mrs Beak took up. 'Some husband returns to his poor deceived wife, telling her that he has been detained about his business, and she, poor innocent, cannot but wonder why he makes such a poor knife and fork when the belated dinner is set before him.'

'Evidently the knife has gone home and the fork has been over-loaded,' Mr Swellington concluded, to Harriet's laughter but the puzzlement of the ladies, who had stomachs as resistant to ribaldry as they were hungry for gossip.

Suddenly, Mrs Muggles clapped her mittened hands. 'I have the strangest fancy in the world! Why do we not, on our return, pass by the Lady Gloria's mansion?'

'To what end?' enquired Mrs Beak, whose quickness of intelligence in the matter of books was not matched by a similar quickness in the matter of worldly commerce.

'There is a poor, bedraggled sort of hedge, that runs beside South Audley Street. 'Tis said that one may peep through it and so espy the dining-room in which the hussy fattens up her victims. 'Twould be an excellent jape to peep through that hedge ourselves!'

'Such a procedure would surely detract from the dignity of two ladies such as ourselves,' Mrs Beak protested.

'We may think of some excuse if anyone should observe us. You may, for example, say that your lap-dog has jumped from the coach and run into the garden and that you are desperate to find it. Or I may say that I am admiring some rare horiticultural specimen. 'Tis well known to all and sundry that botany is all the rage with me.'

Mr Swellington, ever ready for a jape, now joined in: 'Lawks, ladies, the idea is a highly diverting one! Be so kind as to let Danny here and myself accompany you. If your behaviour should elicit any unfavourable comment from the passers-by, we shall be there to defend you.'

'You are very kind, Mrs Swellington. Indeed, I wonder how a lady such as yourself, so decent and proper, can have come to the pretty pass of running such an establishment as this.' Mrs Muggles rose. 'Let us go then! Else I fear that we may be too late and, the meal over, some inamorato will be picking over the carcase in an upstairs chamber invisible to us.'

In a great flutter, the two old hens took wing to the coach, with Mr Swellington and myself in more dignified attendance. You would have thought, from their snickerings and squealings, their nid-nodding and nudging, that they were two young virgins on their first visit to the play.

In the coach, all the talk was still of Lady Gloria: how such as she should set a better example to the commonalty else, all respect gone, the gates of revolution would be flung open wide; that they could not conceive how the good Sir Graham could allow his young wife so much latitude and that either he must be purblind or else he must himself have found some other diversion; how beauty and brains were well enough, but that it was by virtue that we should all come to be judged at the Final Reckoning.

When we arrived in Audley Street, Mrs Beak alighted, to be followed by Mrs Muggles, who was calling out: 'Rufus, come here, sir! Rufus! At once!' I could not conceive what she was about until I suddenly minded me of the pretext of the dog. The two dames ran to the hedge, still calling, 'Rufus! Rufus! Rufus!' so loud that they must have been heard all the way to Piccadilly. Then, on tiptoe, necks craning, they peered through the bosky verdure. I joined them, and through the interlaced branches of privet I saw the beautiful Lady Gloria and, opposite to her at the table, a fat, ugly man who was raising a fork to his mouth.

Suddenly Mrs Muggles let out a scream: ' 'Tis Mr Muggles! Lawks a mercy, 'tis Mr Muggles himself!'

At that she fell to the ground in a swoon.

Mr Swellington and I stooped and raised her supine form, while Mrs Beak called for spirits of ammonia, feathers and sal volatile. In no time at all we were surrounded by just such gapers who, bored with the tedium of their own lives, are ever ready to share in the excitement of the lives of others. One vagrant, an Irishman by his accent, surmised that perhaps the lady was three sheets in the wind; to which a pockmarked harridan, who was hawking whelks, returned that it was obvious to any beholder that, for all her years, she was in the family way. 'Let us transport her to the carriage,' Mr Swellington suggested; and between us we then supported the lifeless woman back across the street.

Having laid her down within the carriage, we ourselves entered it and bade the coachman to drive with all despatch to her house. Her eyelids began to flutter and she emitted one piteous groan on another. Then she sighed, sat up and, swaying from side to side with the accelerating motion of the coach, she began to moan: 'The shame of it! The shame of it! The shame of it!' We knew not what to interpose; but Mrs Beak pressed the poor wretch's hands and Mr Swellington murmured in consolatory tone 'Such, alas, is the lot of us poor women. Men were deceivers ever.' Then Mrs Muggles proceeded: 'To swoon clean away in a public street, before the eyes of so many strangers! I shall never be able to hold up my head again! The shame of it! The shame of it!'

8

In the days that followed, though there were no more extravagant routs, an endless stream of customers passed through the house. More than once some gentleman would make request for my services of Mr Swellington, only to be told that my riding-muscle was still sore from too much pulling. One such gentleman, more importunate than the others, returned disobliging answer that it was *his* custom, when a stallion was spavined, to have done with it and send it to the common market. But if the gentlemen were ill satisfied, the ladies were well sated. Short and tall, fat and thin, dark and fair, lovely and unlovely, young and old: soon such differences were matters of as little emotional import to me as the height of heel, quality of leather and cut of instep to a cobbler. Like him, and like many another honest journeyman, I plied my tool all day and retired to bed tired but contented with the knowledge of a work well done.

One afternoon an exceedingly haughty dame, a French countess, called at the house with a splendid equipage, on the recommendation of the ambassador of her country, one of the regular votaries at that altar of Neptune of which Sam served as high priest. She spoke passably good English, ordering Mr Swellington hither and thither and finding fault with everything that was brought to her or done for her. The chair was too low; the table on which her dish of tea was set was too high; now she felt hot, fanning herself with vigour, and now, calling for a shawl, she felt cold; sipping the tea, she pronounced it, 'Execrable!' but, brought some coffee, she wrinkled her nose in disdain and said that she had yet to drink a passable cup of coffee in this hyperborean wilderness of her exile. When we had gone up to my chamber, she criticized the style and cut of the clothes of which I divested myself; said that my waist was far too narrow and my riding-muscle far too thick; and proclaimed that she could ill support someone of my size on top of her and never cared to lie with another beneath her. My one wish then was to have done with the minx as quickly as I was able; for, though she was formed with an exceptional distinction and grace, I could not abide such contrariness.

Once in my arms (I had decided to compromise by being neither above nor below her but beside her in spoon-fashion) she all at once began to whimper: 'Don't, Danny! Don't! You are causing me hurt!'

I was astounded, protesting: 'But, madam, I have caused you no hurt in the world. Why should I wish to hurt you?'

'Ah!' At that she let out a little scream. 'Why must you be so cruel to me? Why do you wish to punish me in this fashion?'

'Punish you, madam?'

'Is it for my ill-humour? Yes, 'tis true, I am a martyr to ill-humour and, like a child, I am best rid of it if it is beaten out of me. Rid me of my ill-humour, Danny!'

'Madam, I do not comprehend you.'

'You have heard of those who have achieved sanctity by driving out the demons within them with the scourge. I am just such a one. I, too, am possessed of demons, Danny, and you must drive them out. Come, Danny!'

'What is it you wish me to do?'

She had already disengaged her breasts and restored them to the liberty of nature, making me suppose that a new light was added to the room, so superiorly shining was their whiteness. But now, turning over and raising her shift, she displayed to my gaze two posterior globes no less radiant. Chubby, smooth-cheeked and passing fair, they rose cushioning upwards from two fleshful thighs, their cleft a delightful umber. 'I bespoke the instrument of my punishment in advance. Good Mrs Swellington told me 'twould be placed in the closet. Please go look!'

'*This*, madam?' I had opened the closet-door and found therein a birch such as my old tutor had used on me when I had failed in some conjugation or declension.

'Is it springy! Try it, Danny!'

I did as she bade me and answered: 'Yes, 'tis wondrous springy.'

'*Bon!* Then to work!'

'To work?'

'The saints would themselves administer their own flagellation. But I, being connected to many of the crowned heads of Europe, am all unused, as you can see, to hard work, and you must needs do it for me. Come, Danny! Lay on!'

'You really wish me to chastise you, madam?'

'Why else should I have commanded your services at such a high cost?'

'Very well, madam,' I said, wondering what tariff Mr Swellington had set for a task so strange.

At that, I seized the rod and, according to her directions gave her, in one breath, ten lashes with much good-will and the utmost nerve and vigour of arm that I could put into them, in obedience to what we read in *Ecclesiastes* that, 'Whatsoever thy hand findeth to do, do it with thy might.' I had expected her to cry out at such cruelty but she seemed no more concerned than a lobster would at a fleabite. But soon, as lash succeeded lash, skimming the surface of those white cliffs until they were criss-crossed with weals, I was so moved at the piteous sight that, but for the thought of the money that would be lost to Mr Swellington and myself, I would have repented of the undertaking. Now I could perceive that she was wreathing and twisting her body, as an effect not of pain but of some new and powerful sensation; until, on a sudden, she turns over again and cries out, 'Now, Danny! Now! Ravish me! Rive me! Destroy me!' Throwing aside the rod, I needed no further bidding.

Our dalliance over, she was once again the haughty, disdainful, imperious madam, ordering me to hand her now this and now that article of clothing, complaining now that the room was too stuffy and now that she could sense a draught, and exclaiming all the while that she would be late for the play and that the fault was mine.

'I trust you were well satisfied, madam?' Mr Swellington bustled up to ask when we had descended.

'Passing well,' rejoined this Comtesse de la Baguette (for such, she had informed me with an ill grace when I enquired of her, was her appellation).

'Danny always gives satisfaction to my clients,' Mr Swellington retorted, bridling not a little. He pointed to the ledger on the table beside him: 'He is more bespoke in advance than the most eminent of physicians; and I make bold to say that he has cured more ladies of their maladies than any physician in a time so short.'

'I should myself like to bespeak him for this sennight. The Comte –' she pronounced the word in such a way that, having but little French, I at first misunderstood her intention – 'is returning to Paris for a short spell and so I shall find myself at greater liberty and in need of some diversion to banish my melancholy at his absence. I take it that he will be free?'

Mr Swellington consulted his ledger, head on one side and tongue daintily lolling between his teeth, and then said: 'Alas, madam, there is not a free hour all that week. I cannot work him as one would work a pony or a brat down the pit – indeed, I am sure that you would not wish me to do so – and, for his health's sake, more than three tasks in a day I would not wish him to undertake.'

The French madam tapped her foot and bit her lower lip in fury. She was standing, not sitting (though invited to do so) for a reason that was clearer to me than to my employer. 'But I needs must have some diversion while my husband is away. Else I shall succumb to the megrims. I suffer piteously from the megrims in his absence. Surely you may put off some other party in favour of a client such as myself?'

Mr Swellington again bridled, a hectic flush rising up from the less than happy valley over the raddled flesh inadequately covered with a *fichu* of the finest Bogside lawn. ' 'Twould be unethical, madam,' he said.

'My resources are boundless, since my family owns the greater part of Rouen, two bazaars in Pondicherry and some four or five islands of the West Indies.'

Mr Swellington's eyes brightened at this allusion to wealth beyond the dreams of even his avarice. 'Madam, if a business is not conducted with the strictest regard to morality and ethics, then in no time at all it falls into disrepute and ruin. I should greatly wish to oblige you in this matter, as indeed would Danny. But you will acknowledge our dilemma.'

The Comtesse, her cheeks even more flushed than Mr Swellington's front, replied in the most peremptory manner imaginable: 'I can wait no longer. I am already late for the play, as I dally here. Whoever it is that has engaged Mr Hill for this sennight is unlikely to pay what I am ready to pay. Each shilling of your tariff I shall count as a guinea.'

This proposal obviously vanquished all Mr Swellington's moral and ethical scruples at a single blow; but nonetheless he felt obliged to protest: 'I know not what excuse I can offer to the other party, a lady who has patronized this establishment for many a long year.'

'You will be able to find some excuse, I doubt not. You must be skilled in such matters. Why not say that he has pulled his riding-muscle? She needs must accept that.'

'I should not care to be taken in a falsehood; but something I shall contrive. I should not wish for all the world that such a lady as yourself should succumb to the megrims. Such must be my prime consideration. Perhaps Sam or John may play Danny's part, making up in enthusiasm what they lack in inches.'

'Then I shall expect Mr Hill at my mansion at two

o'clock this sennight. Pray do not be late, Mr Hill. I shall retain you for that night at my mansion, that you may sleep well after our diversions.' At that, with a most peremptory tap of her fan on my arm, she spoke her adieus and left us.

Mr Swellington sighed, pursed his lips and then began to amend his ledger, saying: 'When a lady is such a martyr to the megrims, then one must needs do everything in one's power to succour her. Else I should not wish to disappoint our good Mrs Tuohy.' At that, he erased Mrs Tuohy's name with a single stroke of the pen and wrote in, with a flourish: LA COMTESSE DE LA BAGUETTE.

The Comtesse's mansion was far grander than that of Mrs Beak, being replete with costly works of art, a multitude of servants of every age and colour and no less a multitude of dogs of every size and breed. When I remarked on the commodiousness and beauty that I saw on every side, she frowned in most regal fashion and declared: 'To speak the truth, Danny, I am ill pleased with this house, rented off the Duke of M ——— for a sum that would have warranted accommodations rather less pinched and poky. I cannot give a ball for more than two hundred without many a lady succumbing to the vapours because of the overcrowding. Even my servants complain that, instead of sleeping four and five to a room, as is customary, they must sleep six and even seven. The park is hardly adequate for my own exercise (of which more anon), much less that of my Irish Wolfhound.'

After some refreshment, she led me up to her chamber, once again commenting all the while, in a most dis-obliging fashion, on the clothes that I was wearing. How was it, she asked, that Mrs Swellington could allow me out in apparel so unbecoming? It was neither well-fitting nor in fashion. But we should soon remedy that, she went on to assure me.

The room was more like some audience chamber, with acres of lapis lazuli, yards and yards of brocade and damask, and gold and silver gleaming from every corner.

The bed, high piled with cushions of the softest down, was circular and so vast that the Great Bed of Ware itself could not have held candle to it. When I gasped at the size of this bed, the Comtesse informed me that she was the most restless of sleepers and needed much room for manoeuvre, else she fell to the ground.

'Now, dear Danny,' she bid me, abandoning the 'Mr Hill' with which she had addressed me before the servants, 'strip off those unstylish slops of yours, that toggery that would not do credit even to an itinerant tinker, and let us see how you look in these accoutrements but lately come to me from Florence. *Voilà*!' At that she opened a coffer and removed from it the strangest garments that ever I did see. ' 'Tis the latest mode the length and breadth of Italy. Come, try them on!'

The gear that she had produced was all of shiny black leather, with a multitude of studs and bosses of brass. 'I trust that this will not be too small for you,' the French minx said, holding up for my inspection what, at first view, I took to be a muzzle for her Italian greyhound.

I was struck dumb at first; then recovering my powers of speech, I stammered, 'But, madam, I cannot go abroad in clothes such as these. I shall be the laughing-stock of London.'

To this she rejoined: 'We may consider going abroad later. Now you can but try them on. Come!' At that she helped me into a pair of leather trousers, so tight that we must both needs tug with all our might and main, and then into a tunic, mightily strange since two holes had been cut from it at the place where my manly paps might have been thought to need a cover. Fortunately the object she had held up for my inspection was indeed too small for me, your Italian being notoriously bigger of mouth than of riding-muscle. At the last she knelt, though I begged her not to do so, and inserted first one of my feet and then the other into a pair of boots so shiny that you would have thought that they were made of glass.

'Madam, one might suppose that I was about to go to

the chase,' I quipped. To which she answered: 'Indeed, I shall play the timorous hare to your ravening hound.'

When she had risen from the floor, after much polishing of the boots with her hands, she stooped again to the coffer and brought out a mask, it too of black leather. 'Don this,' she commanded me.

'But, madam, if I wear such a thing, I shall look like the common executioner in it.'

'Precisely,' she retorted. 'For you must now be the executioner of both my pain and my pleasure. Come, come sir!' she continued, seeing that I was hesitating. 'Since that apparatus over there –' she pointed with a lily-white hand at the muzzle – 'is too small for us to have one kind of masked ball, let us at least have another.'

Much doubting the sanity of this strange lady, but bethinking me of those guineas that were to be paid instead of shillings, I put on the mask, which I found disagreeably hot and still stinking of the canine cacation with which its leather had been preserved. As soon as it was in place, she threw herself at my feet, crying out, 'Mercy! Mercy! Spare me!' with many an anguished rolling of her eyes and many a heaving of her ample bosom, as she grasped my boots so securely that, had I attempted to move, I should surely have tumbled.

'Madam, what kind of play-acting is this? What mean you? I intend no harm.'

At that she released me and rose to her feet. 'You look so horrendous in that mask that, by my troth, for a moment I was affeared that you had come to make away with me.'

She went over to another coffer, yet larger than the former one, raised the lid and took out of it such an assembly of straps, ropes, cords, chains, inkles and rollers as would have sufficed to secure a whole hulk-load of wretches destined for the penal settlements. 'When my husband is away, I am afflicted by a consuming nervosity,' she explained. 'I twitch, I tremble, I wiggle and wriggle. Like a parched pea, I jump hither and thither. Like a dead leaf, I am agitated with every breath. That I may not dissipate all my vital force in this disorder, you must bind me well.'

'Bind you, madam?'

She went to the bed, lay down upon it, her face in the cushions and those two splendid globes upreared, and then told me yet again: 'Bind me, Danny! Else these paroxysms will prove the death of me.'

'But how shall I bind you to a circular bed, madam? The ropes will have no purchase; the chains will work loose.'

'I have taken thought for all that. Look!' And at that she indicated where some carpenter had cunningly devised catches for the instruments of bondage.

Somewhat loath, I went to work, while the poor wretch kept crying out most piteously: 'No, Danny! No! Do not abstract my freedom from me! Do not make me your prisoner!' But as soon as I desisted, she would urge me on again: 'No, I needs must endure it. 'Tis better for me. Only thus can I be rid of this restlessness that runs through me like a flame.'

Finally, when she had been secured as fast as Andromeda to her rock, she indicated (it was difficult to hear her, since her face was half-obscured by the pillows) that in a third coffer I should find the implements of her punishment and pleasure. I raised the lid and gasped at such a prodigious assemblage of scourges, rods, canes, sticks, rat-tans, quirts, branks, triangles, boots, racks, wheels, iron heels and even an iron maiden. I selected a paddle that was likely to cause her the least anguish and leave the faintest mark and then neared the bed. At my approach, she began to cry out: 'I have sinned, Danny! I have been a wicked and libertine woman! I have used you ill and used the world ill! Do not spare me! Beat the devil from me!'

At that I once again began to thump her; and, indeed, in the exercise I then experienced a growing pleasure. Her posteriors, plump, smooth and prominent, formed luxuriant tracts of animated snow, that splendidly filled the eye. As I struck, it was all again: 'Have mercy! Save me! Help! I repent me of my evil conduct!' and so on and so forth.

It was when I saw the beaded bubbles winking at the brim of her bottom-cavity, that I felt I must desist. 'Madam,' I said, 'I have a most strange horror of any blood. If I see more, then I shall swoon right away.'

'But one or two more strokes!' she begged of me. 'Then I shall have expiated all my wickedness in full.' Thereupon she once again began to writhe with something other than the pain that I had inflicted on her, crying out, 'Danny! Danny! Oh my Danny, oh!' so shrill that I feared that her servants would run in, surmising that some harm to her was afoot.

When I had loosened her ropes and chains, she rose from the bed, gently feeling the seat of her torment. 'Madam,' I said, 'this usage of yours is passing strange.'

'But you must know, Danny, that there is an old wives' saying, "No gains without pains". All that is most pleasurable and most valuable in the world must be brought with rue, torment and affliction. 'Tis the pain that sets the price. Have you never submitted to any such chastisement?'

'Indeed no, madam, except in the way of paying for dereliction or disobedience as a child.'

'Let me prove you then,' said she, snatching up, not the paddle, but a cane, which she began to bend hither and thither between her hands. I hesitated; but then, seeing her in all the magnificence of her imperious nakedness, I consented, 'Very well, madam. As you wish.'

At that she unloosed the tie of my breeches and, with one sharp motion, pulled them down to my knees. Then, viewing my naked posterior globes with great seeming delight, she instructed me: 'Bend over the back of that chair over yon! But take heed that you do not soil it, for the cloth comes from Cathay.' As soon as I had done as I was bid, my knees all a-tremble at the prospect before me, she went on: 'Do not be over-affeared. I shall consider the difference of your sex, its greater delicacy and its notorious incapacity to undergo pain.'

All my back parts, naked halfway up, were now fully at her mercy. First she stood at a convenient distance, rod in hand, delighting herself with a gloating survey of the attitude I stood in. Then, springing eagerly towards me, she covered all those naked parts with a fond profusion of kisses, before she stepped back once more and asked me, 'Ready, Danny?' At that, a thought came to me and fearful of my livelihood, I urged her: 'Have a good care not to strike my twin treasures!' She made no answer to this plea but, taking firm hold of the rod, now began to wanton with me in gentle inflictions on my tender, trembling posterior globes, without in any way greatly hurting them. By degrees, as the lashes became smarter and smarter, I felt an increasing tingling, until I needed all my patience not to cry out or complain at least. You may guess to what a curious pickle those soft flesh-cushions of mine were soon reduced, she now laying into me with a will and now flying to me to kiss away the smart. Many was the time that I all but sprang up, telling her to have done; but a curious pleasure, nay delight, such as I had never experienced before, kept me there, until on a sudden my body was contorted, much like hers on the bed, and I felt the balsamic effusion warm beneath me.

'My chair! My chair! The cloth from Cathay!' With that, she struck me so mightily in her fury that I jumped up, my trousers round my ankles, and snatched the cane from her. 'A little water will rid us of the deed,' I assured her.

'Water!' she shrilled. 'Water will ruin a silk that was woven for the Great Khan himself!'

For a long while she complained about the damage to the chair, about my boorishness and lack of thought and about the pain that so much exercise had given her in the arm. Then brightening on a sudden, she asked me if I wished to go for a tour of the park. When I assented to this proposal, glad of an intermission during which I could recreate my vital forces, she continued, 'But I can see that you are wearied after so much endeavour. You may ride in the chaise.'

'Oh, no, madam!' I protested. 'The park cannot be vast, even by your own admission, and I am well used to walking.' But she insisted that the chaise it must be. Slipping into a shift that seemed to me inedaquate protection against the elements, she led me down to a small winding-stair out of the house and so into a coach-house. 'Pray go up,' she said, indicating an elegant chaise of a style that was either Italian or French and certainly not English.

'But I must needs first place the horse between the shafts,' quoth I.

'The horse may place herself,' she riposted. 'Go up, Danny, do as I bid.'

Much bewildered, I mounted the chaise.

'Is the whip there?' she called.

'Yes, 'tis here.'

'Excellent well.' At that, she threw off her slip, went between the shafts, as naked as a new-born babe, and hauled me out of the coach-house and into the garden. 'The horse cannot trot unless you whip it,' she called; and thus obliged, what could I do but lay on? As the whip struck her lily-white flank, she neighed in a passing good imitation of a high-spirited filly and away we went. Fortunately bosky verdure surrounded all the park, making it impossible for any strange eye to peer or pry into our revels from Park Lane, and not one of her servants was about. Faster and faster we tore round the circuit and louder and louder cracked out the whip. From time to time the evening air was yet again rent by a whinny.

When our sport at last was ended, she was all glistening with sweat. I threw her shift over her and, breathless as she was, I then helped her up the winding stair. 'Now I must bathe myself,' she announced. 'The ass's milk is conveyed hither all the long way from Devon and last week, the autumn being so unseasonably hot, I was told by the Comte that I smelled for all the world like a Camembert cheese. I therefore commanded that it must be kept in the ice-house until such time as I gave orders for it to be drawn. It works miracles for my skin; I have not a single wrinkle. Perhaps you would like to try the same ablution for your treasure-purse?'

'There wrinkles are but natural, madam.'

After her bath was over, she summoned me again to her chamber, where, with the aid of three tiring-women, she was at her toilet. I stood and watched as she upbraided them and they hurried in terror about their tasks, one depilating her legs, one plucking her eyebrows and one affixing the beauty-spot on the corner of her chin. 'You need not lace me,' she said to them, 'for either you lace me so loosely that I am in danger of spilling my fruit or else you lace me so tightly that the fruits are bruised. Mr Hill will lace me. Begone! Away!'

When they had scuttled from the chamber, she rose from her seat and went over to a small box, of gold inlaid with sapphires, that rested on a table among unguents, powders and perfumes. She raised the lid and beckoned me over. 'Do you know what these are, Danny?'

I gazed down and then replied: 'They look mightily like two cow-horns, madam!'

'Cow-horns! These are worth a king's ransom! Indeed, they were given as a ransom when King Mombolele was held captive by a neighbouring tribe of Hottentots and was within an inch of being consumed by them in some sort of heathen hot-pot. These are not your common cow-horns; these are the tushes of rhinoceri!'

'Indeed, I have heard of their miraculous aphrodisiacal power,' I confessed, wishing that I might have at least a part of one to facilitate me in my labours. 'Do you imbibe their powder?'

'Powder! *Sacré dieu!* No, Danny, I use them in a far more efficiacous manner. Sometimes I am content with one, sometimes only two will serve me. Today I shall not be greedy. One must suffice.'

'What are you doing, madam?' She had turned from me, in natural modesty, and, skirt raised, was engaged in some business that I could not observe.

'I am accommodating the tush as is the custom of the Hottentots.' She turned, gave a little wriggle and then smiled on me, replete with satisfaction. 'Do you wish to make use of the other?'

'Thank you no, madam.'

'As you wish. Now we must hurry.'

'Do you intend that I should go abroad in this costume?' I asked, suddenly realizing that I was still accoutred all in leather, with the mask still on my face. It was strange that the tiring-wenches had paid no notice to a gear so extraordinary.

The Comtesse threw back her head and laughed, displaying the whitest set of teeth and the reddest tongue on which I had ever set eyes. 'Lud, no! You will frighten the whole company out of its wits. Lady Gloria will think that, as in olden days, you have come to execute her for being taken in adultery.'

'Lady Gloria!'

'It is to her that we are bidden this evening.' She eyed me sharply: 'Do you know her?'

'No, madam. But I have heard tell of her, of course.'

'No doubt.' She clapped her hands: 'Now hasten, Danny! In your room the valet will have set out all that you are to wear. You may keep the clothes but remember that the jewels are but on loan.'

I was about to quit the chamber, when she summoned me back: 'One moment, Danny! You have not yet laced me! I like to be laced wondrous tight! I can boast of twenty-one inches in the forenoon and twenty-two after dinner.'

'I can boast of almost as many, as you yourself have proved.'

'Please do not remind me yet again of that ruined silk

of Cathay! If I think again on it, I shall succumb to the megrims. . . . Now come and lace me quickly.'

I tugged on her stays, for all the world as if I were attempting to close a trunk overfull of possessions, and all the time she gasped, thrashed hither and thither and threw back her eyes like a landed fish. 'Oh, you will kill me! Ah, I cannot bear it! I cannot breathe!' But as soon as ever I desisted, it was: 'Tighter! Tighter! I must needs have the narrowest waist of all the company.'

In the carriage, the eight spankers rushing us up Park Lane, while the outriders clattered along beside us, I noticed that the Comtesse had become mighty fidgety, shifting from one ham to the other and then back again. At first, I supposed that this to be the effect of her chastisement; but then I minded me of the rhinocerus-tush and surmised that, having secreted it about her person, she must now inadvertently be sitting on it.

Lady Gloria's house was all ablaze with lights and the ladies were all ablaze with jewels. Many more than one of these ladies I had already met under circumstances far more intimate; but I determined to show the utmost discretion. One such acquaintance, the Duchess of P——, whispered to me from behind her fan, when the Comtesse had introduced us to each other as though we were strangers: 'Have no fear, Danny. I shall not sully your reputation. To kiss and tell is not the part of a lady.'

Lady Gloria's gown was cut so low that it seemed as if those two wondrous globes of hers would at any moment burst from their prison for all the world to see. She smiled civilly upon me but, unlike every other woman present, appeared totally uninterested in scanning me for any hidden quality. I was much affronted by this seeming negligence on the part of one who, so far from being as cold and chaste as snow, had the reputation of being Messalina, Phryne, Delilah, Thaïs and Laïs all compounded; and just as 'tis human to crave the fruit that is out of season instead of that which loads the platter, so her very chillness provoked my ardour. In the minuet, the saraband, the rigadoon, the pavane and the gavotte, whether advancing round the crowded dance-floor or seated in some umbratilous nook, my eyes and thoughts were only for her, to such an extent that my companion chided me, 'You are vastly distracted, so that you cannot keep time,' and later, 'I have never known a dancer as stiff as you.'

The Comtesse was still mighty fidgety whenever she sat; but the more she wiggled and wriggled, the more contented her expression. Eventually, Sir Graham Garvice, an elderly and mildmannered gentleman, came up to claim her hand and lead her to the buffet, and I was then able to slip away to seek out Lady Gloria. I found her surrounded by a whole host of dandies and coxcombs, jesting now with one and now making some solemn utterance to another. Sensible that I might provoke her, I nonetheless gathered all my courage and joined her circle. To me she paid no attention and the young blades paid attention to me only to direct sneering or pitying looks at one who was so obviously not of their kind. At a pause in their merriment, however, I bowed to her and said: 'Madam, I would wish to beg of a moment with you alone.'

'Alone!' She looked so scandalized that I began to fear that all the tales that I had heard of her amours might have been so much wind and water. The popinjays of her court looked equally affronted.

' 'Twill take but a minute. I may perhaps be able to impart something to your advantage.'

'I doubt it,' she answered, in voice of niveous gelidity. 'But let us retreat into this nook over here.'

Together we withdrew, the young blades muttering and casting me hostile glances. She settled herself on a sofa and indicated the chair that faced it.

'That your name is Danny I learned when the good Comtesse apprised me of it. I had supposed that she would be coming here with the Comte de Baguette; but I do not object to the substitution. No woman wishes to wear the same gown at every party and so why should we expect her to wear the same escort? Anything else of you, I do not know. What is that you have to impart to me with so much urgency?'

'Lady Gloria, even since I first set eyes on you in the Park, I have been consumed with a passion for you.'

'You are not the first,' she replied in so composed and matter-of-fact a manner that I was thunderstruck, having supposed that the fervour of my words would ignite, whether for good or ill, a similar fervour in her. 'What is it you have in mind?'

'In mind, madam?'

'Do you wish, Mr Hill, to make some practical demonstration of this passion with which you are consumed?'

'Such was my hope, madam,' I began to stammer.

'What is your distinction?'

'I hope that it is already apparent to your eyes.'

Briefly she glanced down. 'Such a testimonial, however lengthy – and I observe that yours is, indeed, voluminous – does not of itself guarantee an engagement with me.'

'But if it is true, madam, as they say, that a good man is hard to find, is it not also true that a hard man is good to find?'

'I have never had any difficulty in finding either the one or the other. What other distinction can you boast?'

'Does not the distinction that I have already cited suffice for you?'

'Far from it. Do you write verses, Mr Hill?' I shook my head. 'Dramatic works?' Again I shook my head. 'Are you a philosopher? A scholar? A musician?' At each of these questions I must perforce again and again shake my head, sensible that I was losing one battle on another. 'Are you likely to become Chief Minister? Lord Chief Justice? Chief-baron?'

This inquisition ended, there was a period of silence. Then she shook her lovely head, her lips beginning to form a smile of faint disdain: 'Then I fear, good sir, that I am not for you nor you for me.'

'But, madam,' I protested, 'what have all these questions to do with the matter as issue? It is not my hand that I am offering you.'

'What has raised this country above all others is the virtue, intellect and ability of its sons. What will preserve it in that state is the continuing production of sons of virtue, intellect and ability. Such is my task. I now have nine offspring, three, alas, female, but six male. Each of the six was sired by a man of the utmost distinction. What you, sir, could bequeath to a son, though it might assure him a life of pleasure, would not also assure his country of a life of service.' She rose. 'Do something big in the world, Mr Hill, instead of merely having something big. Then we may see, we may see.' With this rebuff, all delivered in the most matter-of-fact tone imaginable, she nodded and swept away from me, leaving me in a state of fury and dejection. It was the first time that a locked door had not yielded to my tool and the ignominy of it was bitter.

In the carriage, the Comtesse, now fidgeting even more agitatedly than ever, asked me if I had been diverted by the ball. 'To tell the truth, madam, I found it a little tedious,' I answered her.

'I saw you paying court to Lady Gloria in a private nook. 'Tis there that she first leads her prospective lovers.'

'I have no such prospect before me. Nor would I desire it,' I answered, still smarting from my rejection.

' 'Tis well. For the greatness for which she craves so inordinately, is not a greatness of the kind that you have to offer. She is one of those who is content only if she is bedded by a garter, a laurel-wreath or an ermine robe; to whom no mount of pleasure can bring as much delight as the woolsack; and for whom the reading of some tedious ode or the viewing of some even more tedious play procures more ecstasy that any sweet nothings ever whispered by lover into his mistress's ear.'

When we arrived at the house, still all blazing with

candles, the Contesse enquired of me whether I were fatigued or not.

'A little, madam, to speak the truth. It has been a long day and both of us have travailed much.' (For once, it was the muscle of my arm and not my riding-muscle that was aching after my unwonted exertions.)

'Before we retire to bed, let us revivify ourselves with a little music.'

'Music, madam?'

'I am great lover of music. Let us go to inspect my organ.'

'Alas, I have no aptitude for the keyboard. At best, I can bear my part in a round.'

But she did not heed me. 'Come!' she commanded, beckoning me down a passage-way. 'This organ has but lately been assembled. It was made for me in Switzerland by one of the most cunning of clockmakers and fashioners of automata. After my dear friend the Marquise de L—— was taken to her maker, this man fashioned a doll in her image, so lifelike that her husband knew no difference and her lover barely so. This organ is one of the wonders of the world. My husband had to pay for it a sum so large that I tremble to name it to you.'

'He is then fond of music, madam?'

'Not in the least! It is because he cannot share this passion of mine, that he gave orders for this organ to be constructed. It was many years in the building.'

We had now entered what the Contesse termed the music-room; to my simple eyes it was more like a church, with its spacious tunnel-vaulted nave, penetrated by clerestory windows, its air of solemn hush and the appearance, raised on a dais at the farthest end, of what looked much like an altar. Taking my hand in hers, she led me up into the organ-loft. 'But, madam, as I have told you,' I protested as we were climbing, 'I have no skill in playing. Would that it were otherwise, but I cannot but speak the truth!'

'You will learn quickly. 'Tis the easiest thing in the world.'

'And who shall blow for us? Must we summon one of the servants?'

'There is a water-mill hard by, fed by the effluent of the Fleet. The Swiss most cunningly harnessed its power to fill a series of bellows. All you must needs do is tickle the keys.'

'And will you not also play, madam.'

'No, I shall repose me, as I listen to the strains that you wring from the instrument.'

We had now entered the loft and had approached the keyboard. It looked passably like the keyboard of any other organ, until I gazed more closely. Then I saw that the stops, instead of carrying such descriptions as *'vox humana'*, 'diapason,' 'clarinet,' *'voix céleste'* and so forth, instead bore in Latin the names of various parts of the human anatomy viz. *'pes'*, *'mons veneris'*, *'manus'*, *'membrum virile,'* *'scapula'*, *'tibia'*, *'papilla dextra'*, *'papilla sinistra'*, etc. There were fewer keys than on an ordinary organ and these too had descriptions written on them, likewise in Latin: being the names of various implements of torture and chastisement, such as: rod, cane, pincer, piercer, thumbscrew, razor, bistoury, bodkin, etc. As I stood marvelling, she bid me, with some impatience, to mount the stool. 'I shall go below,' she continued, 'and lay me down so that I may enjoy the harmonies of pleasure and pain to best advantage.'

'But how shall I know which keys to strike and which stops to open?'

'Let your hands rove as they will. Do not be afraid that you will mark me, for it is the special power of this instrument that it transmits the most exquisite of sensations without in any way harming the human body. Thus, you may, for example, pull out that stop marked 'naso' and yet my own nose, though it may suffer the greatest torment, will remain in its pristine state of loveliness. Come! Let me descend and then you will begin!'

She hurried down the stairs, with a great rustle of her

hooped skirts, so extreme was her eagerness to be started. I watched, looking down, as she approached the altar, stripped herself and then, *in puris naturalibus*, lay supine on it, her lovely black hair trailing down to the ground and her no less lovely thighs gleaming up at me. She smiled and motioned me to start.

I pulled out '*papilla sinistra*' and then touched the key marked 'pincer'; and though I could hear nothing, I observed how at once she began to writhe and wriggle in what was both an anguish and an ecstasy. Now, as I pulled both '*anus*' and '*mons veneris*' at one and the same moment and then let my fingers fall on 'cane' and 'cat-o'-nine-tails' the poor wretch threw herself about as though in a conniption. Feeling pity for her, I quickly pulled out '*manus*' and then gave to 'tawse' a gentle vibrato; but ill satisfied with such leniency of treatment, she called out, 'Louder! Louder!' Soon I had run the whole gamut of stops and keys and, horrified by the sufferings of the poor woman, even though she herself had sought them, I should have given over, had I not bethought me that my profession would soon lose some of its dignity if supposed to be over-nice.

At long last (by now my hands, unused to playing, were aching as much as her limbs) she rose up off the altar and commanded me to halt. 'Never did Mr Bach compose a fugue of such heavenly dimensions. 'Tis said that the greatest art is that which is the closest to a mirroring of nature. The symphony that you have just played on me was a true work of art in such respect. Nature is both cruel and benign, both destroying and healing, as prodigal of pain as of pleasure. You are indeed a master!'

'I fear that I played indifferent well, madam,' I replied with becoming modesty in answer to such eulogy. 'I have no natural bent and no practice.'

'You played like an angel – and devil.'

When we had once more regained her chamber, she directed me that I was to sleep in the vast round bed beside her, adding to my dismay: 'But I sleep wondrous badly,

Danny. So remember: do not touch, do not toss, do not snore.'

'Lying so near unto someone so beauteous, 'twill be difficult to obey that prohibition.'

'Yet you must needs do so. Our revels now are ended.'

You may imagine what kind of night I then passed, so near to one of the loveliest of forms that I had ever set eyes on and yet forbidden to make any move. Those breasts alone, bare in their pride and whiteness to the moonlight, seemed to plead with my hands to rove; and when I glanced down to that pink slash in the glossiest white satin, I began to tremble as with a fever. Slowly, moving myself inch by inch so that I should not rouse her, I began to approach; but as soon as my thigh alighted on hers, she gave a little start and bade me, in the most imperious voice, to move over and mind my manners. Sleep was then impossible for me and I lay, rigid and miserable, until such time as the dawn shone through the curtains and I could hear the servants going about their matutinal duties. At long last, my lady woke; sat up in the bed, her bubs all bare and her hair all dishevelled; and then turned about and stared at me as though I were some intruder whom she had never seen before. 'What do you here?' she demanded.

'Madam, I have been sleeping or endeavouring to sleep.'

' 'Tis no wonder that my repose was so fitful and crowded with evil dreams. Be up and begone!'

'Now, madam?' I asked, not at all loath to be up but not wishing to be gone until I had consumed at least a dish of chocolate to revive my powers.

'Instanter! If you have need of any sustenance you may take it with the servants! Come, sir! Do not incommode me longer!' Conscious now of those gleaming globes of hers, at which I had been staring, she pulled the sheet up to cover them, with what was the most petulant of gestures. 'Do not gaze at me so! I am no object in a peep-show!'

'Forgive me, madam!'

'Make haste!'

I jumped out of bed and began to busy myself with my toilet, while she herself never ceased to upbraid me for my lethargy and incompetence – my hose was not rightly pulled up, I had omitted a topmost button, my shoes were muddied over. Then, when I was ready to take my leave of her, she jumped from the bed, pulling the sheet round her. 'You have not taken with you any of the jewels that were set out for your wear?'

'Indeed no, madam. I remembered your injunction.'

'Turn out your pockets?'

'Madam!' I was scandalized.

'Turn out your pockets; else I will summon my major domo!'

At that I needs must do what she bid, for fear of causing a scandal.

'Good,' she said, having come on nothing other than some small coins, a kerchief and one of the old woman's little purses. 'Then you may leave me.'

'As you wish, madam,' I said in the most dignified and coldest tone that I could muster.

'But stay!' She had now crossed over to a box, similar to that in which she had kept the rhinoceros tushes. She opened it and took out a bag, that clinked as she moved with it towards me, her lily-white arm upraised. 'I shall send my major domo to settle my score personally with that evil hussy of yours. But this is for your own pains; and for mine.'

In amazement, I took the bag from her, feeling it heavy in my palm.

She gazed at me for a moment and then she said: 'Doubtless, Danny, you have imagined that all these hours it is you who has played the master to me and I who have played your slave. The truth is quite other. You have not degraded me, since it was my will, not yours, that you should use me as you did. I have done what I have wanted; and I have persuaded you to do what you did not want. I found pleasure in my pain; you found only pain in my pleasure. Last night you did not possess me, though lying so close; and you will never possess me again. The money that is in your hands is the proof that it is you who **are** my minion, not I yours. She who pays the piper calls the tune; and it was indeed a merry tune that you played for me on my organ – the tune of my calling.' At that she gave me a push, as though she detested me, and I found myself falling through the door and then down the stairs, while she stood laughing above me. The servants below, evidently used to such happenings, paid no attention to my descent nor to my subsequent tidying of my person but, without deigning even to raise their eyes, continued with their sweeping and scrubbing.

9

Every occupation, however pleasurable and profitable, must eventually begin to pall. 'What!' the gentle reader will exclaim. 'You were performing the task for which the Maker might expressly have formed you and which most men would rather perform than any other; you were being paid for the performance; and yet you wearied of it?' To this impeachment, I can but answer, 'Yes.' There dawned a day when I awoke and looked forward to the duties ahead of me not with agreeable expectation but with indifference. It did not signify one iota that my first customer was a beautiful young heiress, married most unsatisfactorily to a phthisic baronet incapable of carrying out his marital duties; nor that my second was a plump widow, strong of wind and limb, who had served so long as a votaress of Aphrodite Pandemos that I had learned from her many Cyprian mysteries previously hidden from me. The thought of neither could arouse me; only their actual presence could do so and then but slowly.

Later, there dawned another day when I awoke, not in a state of indifference, but in one of positive reluctance, like that of some skivvy who faces the prospect of yet another day of rubbing and scrubbing. 'I have a mighty fine list for you this morning,' Mr Swellington greeted me, opening his ledger and running down the names. But for all my enthusiasm he might have been some exacting mistress giving instructions for broom and brush. No longer could the prospect of snowy thigh, of opulent globes, whether anterior or posterior, or even of that delicious cleft itself bestir me from my sluggishness. Only one thing could now do that; the thought of the money that was increasing for me, like some well-watered tree, under Mr Swellington's careful husbandry. Often now was the time when, instead of breathing those words that provoke in the lover a yet wilder frenzy, I would find myself murmuring over and over again to myself, 'Money, money, money.' More than once the then object of my attentions would catch this barely audible incantation and would ask of me in some bewilderment, 'What was that, my dearest dear?' to which I would reply that 'money' was but another form, in the newest cant of the day, for 'treasure' or 'precious'.

Mr Swellington noticed my lethargy, wan looks and lack of eagerness and began to fear, as well he might, for the health of the silly goose (as I later, in retrospect, saw myself to have been) who laid his golden eggs. He suggested that I might perhaps care to take the invigorating air of Brighthelmstone, where he had some gentleman acquaintances who, he was sure, would be delighted to assume the care of me. Next, he proposed the waters of Bath, sovereign for every kind of mopes, mumps and spleen. Finally when a customer complained of the slowness with which I had brought her to her journey's end and my seeming indifference as to whether she ever arrived there or not, he offered me some Spanish concoction that, as he put it to me, would soon sharpen my quill. But, having all my life had a horror of all nostrums, boluses and Galenicals, I refused with vigour. 'Let me then, Danny,' the creature went on, 'subscribe you in my other ledger. I know that you have little taste for what I myself term the fairer sex but that you would term the stronger one; but if, for a brief period, you were able to adapt yourself to a role of subservience, you would soon be able to recreate your vital fluids. I have many a generous, kindly gentleman who, bent on his own pleasure, will not concern himself with whether you have also achieved your own.' But such a proposal was repugnant to me and I indignantly rejected it.

John, like myself, was also fretting and often spoke to me, in secret, of his wish to leave the establishment, to set up some small business of his own with the monies that lay to his account and then to redeem his Hetty from her pot-house. 'Why do you not come with me, Danny?' he would ask; to which I would return that perhaps next week I should indeed take my departure. The truth was that, each time that I thought of the money that I had already gained by my exertions, I at once thought of the monies that I was in the way to gaining. John also urged on me the wisdom of a change of custom – ' 'Tis nothing to it, Danny. At first a little pain; later, nought but a little discomfort. 'Tis even said that 'tis a remedy wonderfully efficacious in the case of the piles.'

To which I retorted, with much vehemence: 'I do not have the piles!'

At last, with or without me, John decided to bid adieu to our trade. ' 'Tis said that there is no shame greater than that of the fallen woman,' he told me, in apprising me of this resolve. 'But I have become increasingly sensible of the shame of being a fallen man. Surely redemption through love is not impossible even to one who has sunk as low as I?' But when he went to inform our employer that he wished to quit a life of sin and asked that the accumulated earnings of that sin should be made over to him, Mr Swellington would not accommodate him, making many an excuse yet again about the money being out in funds and not for the present being recoverable without much difficulty and the possibility of loss. John became importunate, even accusing Mr Swellington, who was now obdurate in his refusal, of having diverted the money to his own use. High words were exchanged, with Harriet joining in, extremely shrill, on the part of his master, until John struck him, at which the poor wretch succumbed to a fit of the hysterics, Rarely had our house been so convulsed!

If Mr Swellington refused to yield up John's earnings to him, might not he treat me in the same fashion? How

144

true it is that we most often become indignant over the plight of another, when we realize that that plight might be our own. Thus it was that, John sulking in his room with many a threat that, by G—d, he would have the law on the d——d scurvy knave and Harriet sobbing his heart out on the bosom of the ancient cook with many a, 'To use a maid in so barbarous fashion!' etc., etc., I descended to remonstrate with our patron. Unfortunately he was about to receive a whole troop of guests and some of the irregulars – Irish guards, reeking of poteen, tobacco and damp boots – were already in the drawing-room. 'What is it, Danny?' he asked me in a voice so haughty that I supposed that he had already surmised what it was. 'I trust that you are prepared for our revels of the evening?'

'Sir,' I replied, 'before I take part in any revels, I must have your assurance that, at any moment that I may so desire it, you will yield over to me the accumulation of my earnings.'

'I do not care for this peremptory tone; and I do not care to be addressed as "sir" instead of "madam". Your earnings are safely in my keeping.'

'I must remind you that I have never received any account of them.'

'Do you then mistrust my honour?'

'Honour is not something in which a man may ever put much trust. I desire my monies now.'

'Now?'

'Instanter!'

Mr Swellington threw back his head and laughed, stretching his wattles like some turkey tilting up its beak. 'You are not so simple, Danny, country lad though you are, to imagine that I keep here, on these premises, money that any of those rascals next door would cut my throat to abstract from me.' He indicated, with a shake of his towering wig, the guards at their merriment in the next-door chamber. 'But all is well secured. Do not fret or fear.'

'May I have your word then that, tomorrow, you will let me have all monies in full?'

Mightily displeased, my patron began to argue with me as he had already argued with John; and when I still persisted, it was not long before he became abusive of me, calling me ingrate, jackanapes, jessamy, nidget, dizzard, noddy and many another opprobrious term that our clients would have been appalled to hear from the lips of a 'lady' so fine. I regret that I retaliated, countering with appellations hardly less insulting, such as rock, falcon, shark, harpy. It was when, in an access of rage, I called him 'Greek', that he kicked out at me with his Milan slipper, striking me on the shin with such force that I was driven to retaliate by knocking off his wig to reveal his bald pate. John had by now run down the steps to join me in my objurgations, with cries of 'Picaroon! Thimble-rigger! Moss-trouper!' In no time at all the three of us were rolling hither and thither on the floor, in a most un-gentlemanly (and, indeed, unladylike) disorder, that did no credit to a house in which the rules of propriety and decorum had always been so strictly observed. I was entangled in Mr Swellington's panniers and he, in turn, was entangled in John's fob-chain; John and I were pushing and punching and our patron was spitting and scratching. (As I recollect this unedifying scene, I cannot but feel shame for it, however great the provocation.) Then, at the top of his voice, Mr Swellington was shrilling: 'Sam! Sam! Help!'

Naked to the waist (he had been dressing for the revels) Sam came leaping down the stairs, like some pirate about to board a captured hulk, his tattoos all a-flashing and his muscles all a-ripple. 'Summon those poltroons to our aid!' Mr Swellington screamed to him. But the guards, foaming tankards in their hands, had already been drawn away from the buffet by the noise and the scent of a battle. In a trice, they had joined the mêlée, flinging tankards aside and striking and kicking each other and even Mr Swelling-ton when they were unable to strike and kick the hapless

John and myself. Battered and bruised, the blood trickling from our noses and mouths, we were finally flung out, like two sacks of ordure, into the courtyard, with many a boggish jeer and imprecation and many an instruction not to show our d——d faces in that neighbourhood again. Harriet, who had held aloof, now rushed out into the courtyard, where we lay groaning and moaning under a full moon, and kicked each of us in that seat both of man's greatest pleasure and of his greatest pain, shrilling meanwhile: 'Begone! Away! Do not soil a decent house!'

Slowly, with great difficulty and anguish, we gathered ourselves. 'We must have the law on them,' John muttered as he felt the place where an eyetooth once had been.

'We must have revenge on them, certainly,' I retorted, 'but I fear that this is not now either the time or place. As for the law, it will not care to discriminate between us, villains all in its purblind eyes. If we invoke its might, in no time at all we shall find ourselves in the hold of some rat-infested carrack on our way to the penal settlements.'

John soon acknowledged the widsom of my answer. The seat of his breeches was split, his shirt was torn and he was missing, not only the eyetooth, but also a hank of hair. I was in hardly a better case, one eye almost closed from the impact of an Irish fist and one nostril already closing from a congelation of blood.

Supporting each other, we wandered out into the night; and as wretches will always do, however hopeless the prospect before them, we sought to find some consolation.

'At least, we have said farewell to a filthy trade,' John said. ' 'Tis better to be honest, if poor.'

I was not myself entirely convinced of this, else why should the world be so full of poor but honest people striving to become rich and dishonest ones? But I had not the heart to argue with my comrade at that moment.

'We do not need such as Mr Swellington,' I took up. 'We can conduct our own commerce without such an intermediary.'

' 'Twill be mighty strange to live a god-fearing life after that sinful life of ours all these months past.'

I all but retorted that it would be, not only mighty strange, but also mighty difficult; but seeing my comrade spitting blood into the gutter out of that gap between his teeth, I again took pity on him and forbore.

'I have a few coins in my pocket,' I said. 'How say we take some food and drink while pondering on our future?'

'I know not if I am in a fit condition to eat; but to drink I am certainly able. Alas, my pockets are empty. But in due course I shall make restitution to you for any monies you expend on my behalf.'

I might have guessed (but did not do so) that John would lead me to the pot-house, an evil-smelling place among the stews of Blackfriars, where his Hetty worked. She was seated on the knee of a peg-legged mariner in a dark corner of the shop but, seeing us enter, she jumped up and hurried over to us with many an exclamation of pity for our condition. I did not desire any too close a proximity to the wench, being mindful of the infection that she had passed to poor John, and was glad that it was on his knee that she now perched herself, her blubbery arms about his neck and her bosom, all but bursting from the constriction of her bodice, heaving upon him. She looked like a country-wench (and indeed her speech so betrayed her), with a high colouring, thick hair and hands that looked strong enough to coax milk from the driest or most obstinate of teats. She asked most frankly about John's indisposition and said that she herself was now mended or at least supposed herself to be so, since she had had no customer complaining of late. After many a jar of ale, both John and I began to feel weary and bethought us where we could lie for that night; whereat the wench said that we were welcome to make use of her chamber, if we were not too much averse to her snoring, something that she was told that she did to excess. For lack both of money and vital force, we consented readily to this suggestion and were then shown by her to what was little more than a kennel, ankle-deep in straw, in the yard of the pot-house. Having removed the greater part of her clothing, which was soiled with grease, wine and who knows what else, and preparing to join her John in a corner, the kindly wench bethought herself that mayhap I should like a companion for the night; and added that, in such a case, Riggish Doll might be available; but I demurred, telling her that the only arms in which I now wished to lie were those of Morpheus. I know not whom, in her ignorance, she imagined Morpheus to be, but she gazed at me much askance before bidding me goodnight.

On the morrow, John was far jollier than I. I had woken at the first crow of the cock, the other two still snoring in swinish slumber beside me after their strident exertions of the night, and had then lain thinking, with much heaviness of heart, of the life and the earnings both now forfeited to me. I forgot, as a man inevitably does when a greater misfortune succeeds a lesser one, all that I had suffered, working all those months as Mr Swellington's gull, and instead thought only of my commodious chamber, so different from this hovel of straw and filth; of the elegant clothes that I had been obliged to leave behind me; of the savorous repasts prepared by the old cook; and, above all, of all the women, fair and dark, young and old, thin and fat, short and tall, whose acquaintances I had made in the way of business. Then I began bitterly to reproach myself, with reminders that even the life of a King Emperor must be largely a routine; that to jump out of a luxurious frying-pan into a scorching fire is always the height of folly; and that now, after something near to a year, I was exactly where I had started on my arrival in London.

'Is't not fine to be leading an honest life once again?' John demanded of me when he had disentangled himself from Hetty's embraces and despatched her to see what comestibles she could forage for us.

Shivering and hungry, every bone in my body aching from my beating of the night before and my fine clothes all now tattered and filthy, I could not share in his enthusiasm and merely nodded sadly.

John continued: 'I feel like some Hottentot slave who is on a sudden given his freedom.'

I thought that I should prefer at that moment to be given my breakfast; but when the wench returned, it was with nought but a crock of milk, soured and therefore intended by her mistress for the pigs, and a quartern-piece of bread filched by her from the bin, so hard and green with age that I could hardly get my teeth into it. However, I thanked her most civilly. She was a good soul and could not be blamed for the way in which the world had used her country innocence and for the way in which she had learned to use the world. When John retired to the jakes, a lean-to at the other end of the courtyard, she became mighty winsome and asked me how it was that John had never brought me to the pot-house with him before. I replied that I did not greatly frequent the pot-houses, to which she replied that she could see that I was a true gentleman and that there was nothing dearer to her heart than a gentleman who was truly a gentleman. As she spoke all this, she was busily eyeing me, her mouth open to reveal a fine set of large, white teeth, while with one hand she scratched under an arm-pit (indeed, I myself had been pestered and bothered by fleas all through the night) and with the other somewhere else. 'John is a good man,' she went on, 'but he has not that gentlemanly quality that I find in you. I have a nose for a gentleman —' at this she touched that organ with a grubby forefinger – 'however low he may have fallen and however seemingly impenetrable his disguise. Beshrew my heart but I pity you, my poor Danny, since you must needs have fallen far now to lie so low. We are two of a kind. I (though it must remain a secret between us) am the daughter of one, a nobleman of great consequence, whose name I must not speak. Undone by his brother, my uncle, I was cast out into the snow, my belly big with child. The child deceased and I myself all but deceased. Then I found employment with the good people who keep this house. 'Tis not the life to which I was accustomed, but I needs must make the best of it.' Through all this artless nonsense, that none would believe even if he were to read it in one of Lady Gloria's romances, she approached nearer and nearer unto me, until one hand was toying with the tendrils of my hair (no doubt making them even more greasy and dirty than heretofore) and was about to toy with me elesewhere, I the while praying that whatever stricture was detaining John in the jakes would speedily resolve itself. Fortunately he returned before I must needs repulse the wench and so earn that enmity that invariably springs up in the bosom of any woman scorned.

John was now full of plans for work with an uncle of his, a mason who lived not far off in Kennington. 'He is but a mason in a small way of business,' he declared, 'and any wage that we earn will be small in consequence. But at least the wage will be an honest one and we shall be earning our livings by the sweat of our brows.'

I forebore to ask what difference there was between earning one's living by the sweat of one's brow or by an effusion from some other place and, having bid a farewell to the good but draggle-tailed Hetty, I set off with him to walk the two or three miles to his uncle's abode.

This uncle, though all along the way John told me that he was the kindest, gentlest, most generous, best sort of man in the world, seemed markedly lacking in gladness to receive us. He reminded John that, despite the many months that he had spent in the city, this was but his first visit; adding that in the case of some people want was a sharper spur than duty. Business was bad, he continued, he must needs find a dowry for his still unmarried daughter, else no one would ever take her off his hands; and we looked too fine a couple of gentlemen to stoop to the kind of ill-paid drudgery that he could offer us. To this John replied, with more eagerness than I myself could muster, that, provided the work were honest, the heaviness of its labour and the lightness of its recompense were alike of little moment. His uncle seemed better satisfied with this answer than anything that passed between us heretofore and gave instructions to his daughter Ida (whom he habitually addressed as 'girl', though she must have passed far beyond her thirtieth summer) to show us our accommodations. These proved to be one small and chilly room tucked under the eaves, with no furniture other than two trestle-beds, two chairs and a plain, unpolished table. When we descended to eat, the repast was no less spare.

In the days that followed John carried as many a hod as he had ever laid sod in the past; and I worked as briskly with the trowel as I had ever worked with any other tool. The honest sweat, in which John had taken such pride, certainly ran down off our foreheads; but its honesty seemed less and less of a compensation for the hardship of our lot. We fed poorly and we slept deeply; our hands became calloused and our brains addled. What money he received, a pitiful sum, John would spend on his Hetty; but there were others who spent more and she was hoity-toity with him. What money I received, a sum no less pitiful, I first used to accoutre myself in clothes less tattered and torn and then laid aside in the hope that some day I should amass enough to start some business of my own. Even John's spirits began to droop and decline; and I myself was so much wearied at the close of each day that I had no taste for the dalliance that had once been my chief pleasure in life – no, not even on those occasions when the opportunity presented itself in the pleasing form of some serving-wench or the less pleasing one of my employer's daughter.

This last had all too evidently taken a prodigious liking to me. More than once I had caught her peeping through the window of the wash-house when I was at my ablutions and through the window of the jakes when I was at my matutinal exercise. She would offer to mend the rents in my clothes, to sew on lost buttons and to wash my linen for me. At our frugal mealtimes she would find occasion to brush against me as she set down the dishes, would seek out my knee under the table with her bony ones and would surreptitiously offer me the pope's nose. Such was her ugliness that I maintained a total indifference to all these manifestations of affection.

It soon became apparent to me that John was not dealing wholly sincerely with his uncle. If we were left to labour alone at our plastering and painting, he would at once down tools and betake himself either to slumber or to the nearest pot-house. He would stint on timber, nails, lime, bricks and such like, no doubt to the future detriment of the houses that we were raising or repairing, and would then sell what he garnered in this fashion to some purchaser more concerned with price than with provenance. The peculations were petty and the gains therefore small; but he was thus enabled to buy his Hetty some pinchbeck finery from week to week and so keep himself in her good graces, even if he could not assure to himself the sole enjoyment of her favours. When I remonstrated with him on such conduct to one who was not merely his employer but also the brother of his mother, he retorted that if an employer used his servant with less than honesty, then the servant had the right to be less than honest in return. 'But how is your uncle less than honest with us?' I then queried. 'He pays what he promised to pay and has in no way reneged on our original contract.'

To this John answered: 'Forsooth, if he does not pay us enough, then he cheats us! And if he cheats us, then we may cheat him back! 'Tis obvious.' But the logic of this, although unanswerable, nonetheless left me uneasy.

Alas, the inquisitive Ida, no doubt following our comings and goings with more assiduity than either of us suspected and no doubt also searching about among our possessions when we were gone from our room, eventually became apprised of what John was doing; and one evening, after an Irish stew containing naught but potatoes and barley and some slivers of mutton-bone, she came to us, on the pretext of returning some darned hose of mine, to divulge what she knew. John was flabbergasted and mightily afraid, even going down on his knees on the rank and wretched straw of our chamber to beg her not to communicate her discovery to her father, else all would be over for us. At best he would drive us forth from the house; at worst, he would inform the law of our knavish conduct and we should find ourselves in no time at all in the stocks or on the high seas. I did not care greatly for this 'our' and 'we', since I had had no part at all in the dishonesty and, indeed, had protested to him of it. But I forbore to intervene.

Hands on hips, the buxom hag surveyed him as he cringed on the floor before her. Then, with much disdain, she told him that she knew that I was but a poor innocent and that he should be ashamed to attempt to embroil me in his evil doings. Then she went on: 'If you were here alone, despite the cousinship between us, I should myself inform against you to the law and take pleasure in doing so. But since you are fortunate to have such a pretty and agreeable gentleman for your companion, I am prepared to relent on one condition.'

John rose from his semi-recumbent posture as this possible dawn began to break over the sea of his troubles and queried in a voice grown reedy with apprehension what this condition might be. Bold as brass, with not so much as a blush or a maidenly lowering of the eyes, she pointed at me, declaring: '*That!*' I thought for a moment that it was mighty discourteous of her to refer to me with no more ceremony than this pronoun; but then I realized that what she was indicating was not me *in toto* but merely a part of me.

'Odzookens, madam!' I cried out. 'What can you mean?'

'It must be clear to you what I mean, dear Danny. Have I not given every indication these past nine weeks, three days and eleven hours that I have a preternatural craving for you? Are you so deaf and blind? Did I not, but yesterday, press the pope's nose on you under the table?'

'But, madam, I could not serve your father so ill as to serve you in the fashion you desire.'

'Your friend here has served my father ill enough.'

I continued to protest that my loyalty to her father and my regard for her maidenly modesty both precluded any agreement on my part to her proposal, but she was as hard as the black bread with which we had but lately eked out the niggardly Irish stew. 'Both for the love in which I hold my father and for my high regard for probity, I can feel nothing but emotions of shock, horror and disapprobation at the opprobriousness of your conduct. You may either exacerbate those emotions or placate them. I leave it to you, gentlemen. Tomorrow, at this selfsame hour, I shall present myself here. Danny has the means wherewith to stop my mouth.'

At this she left us.

'John!' I cried out. 'Now see the pass to which your conduct has brought me! Did I not protest to you that you would be undoing of us? I can see that the raddled witch is set on having her pound of flesh; and I am no less set on not giving it to her.'

John began to plead with me, all but going down on his knees as he had done to the imperious Ida. 'Twas true, he said, that outwardly her appearance was less than seductive; but he warranted that the most wanton and provocative fires coursed within her. 'Twas true, also, that the first bloom of youth had faded, never to be recalled; but a woman, like a tree, must be valued as much for the fruits of her autumn as for the blossoms of her spring. For one such as me, so vigorous and manly, it was but a little labour to grant her her desire. Had I not done as much for a host of women even more ill-favoured, during my service with Mrs Swellington?

All the next day, as we went about our work or I went about it and John took his repose, he continued to argue and plead with me. Now it was all: How could I not do a service to an old friend who had done me a service by finding me employment? If he were cast out, then it was like that I too should share his fate, since it was on his recommendation that I had been engaged. If he were consigned to the rigour of the law, then was it not probable that I, for all my protestations of innocence, should be regarded as his accomplice?

At last, wearied and overborne, I must needs give my reluctant assent.

After we had supped, Ida came into us, as she had promised. She had had the decency to wash at least her face and had laced herself into as tight a bodice as you could ever hope to see. 'Well?' she demanded, hands again on her ample hips. 'Are you gentlemen decided?'

It was John who spoke up: 'My good friend is delighted to comply with your conditions.'

At that he stretched himself on his bed with the daily scandal-sheet and she pushed me over on to mine, throwing herself on top of me with a neigh of pleasure, as of some demented she-ass.

'Madam,' I protested, 'I cannot proceed as long as there remains a witness in this room.'

John looked up from the scandal-sheet, which was no doubt concerned with the further doings and undoings of Lady Gloria, and told us, as cool as you please, that he was so much absorbed in his reading that what we did between us was a matter of indifference to him. However, on my declaring that as long as he remained closeted in the chamber, my manly vigour would remain closeted in my breeches, he finally rose with a very ill grace and made his way to the jakes. The final obstacle being thus removed I needs must, willy nilly, perform my duty.

The happy valley was a veritable chasm; the cleft a veritable cock-pit. Never had I endured such a thrashing and clashing, such a plucking and sucking, such a bestriding and riding. The sweat, flowing freely off her, stuck us together like two limpets. . . . But I dare not shock the sensibilities of the gentle reader with a full description of all that passed between us. Let me only say that this female Shylock was not only determined to have the whole pound of flesh but to swallow every morsel of it. It was a long time before John could return, shivering, from the jakes.

Then there followed the most cruel eleven days that ever I passed. 'Tis said that the appetite grows in the feeding and now this monster was insatiable. True, she plied me with every imaginable delicacy, both as a demonstration of her affection and in an attempt to preserve my strength. But this could not recompense me for a traffic so degrading. Often I pleaded with her to have done but she would none of it, saying that, without this distraction, her better feelings would inevitably assert themselves and she would feel obliged, for reason of the love she bore for her father and for probity and honesty, to tell all. This 'all' now also included the consideration that I had stolen the shrivelled cherry from her orchard; a theft for which her father might well demand matrimony as expiation.

At last the night came when I felt that I should rather serve out my sentence in the penal settlements than on her person and I apprised John of my decision. To my astonishment, he now made no demur or protest. 'You are right, Danny,' he told me. 'For a man to be held in thrall to a woman is neither decent nor proper. I am myself minded to quit this establishment.'

I was dumbfounded. 'But how shall you manage?' I asked of him. 'And what if your uncle has recourse to the law?'

'I plan to make for Bristol city, where there is many a tar who, after a long abstention, will pay highly for the commodity that I shall sell him.'

My mouth fell agape. 'But I thought, good John, that you had forsworn the life of a gentleman of easy virtue.'

'So I have! So I have! Pray do not misunderstand me! What I propose is to take my good Hetty along with me and there to open a shop with her. I am a generous man, not given to jealousy. What I enjoy, I am willing to cede for the enjoyment of others. Fortunately, such is the constitution of a woman that she may make many more men happy in a single day than any man can make women.'

I sank on to my bed, my head in my hands. Then I looked up and said: 'But you have so often railed against such as Mr Swellington and your uncle who cheat those in their employ by using them as chattels?'

At this he looked excessively pained. 'But, Danny, I do not intend to cheat my Hetty. How could I cheat one who is so dear to me? Nor should I cheat you, if (as I sincerely hope) you will come to work for me?'

'I?'

'There are tastes such as Hetty, for all her ardour, skill and willingness, cannot satisfy. There is many a rich merchant in Bristol city and many a discontented wife waiting for that merchant to return from his counting-house or store-house. The pickings will be easy and substantial.'

'You are very good, John,' I rejoined with a sarcasm that I could see to be lost on him. 'But I do not wish to work for any other man but only for myself. If I ply a trade, be it that trade or some trade more respectable, 'twill be on my own account. I am mighty sensible of the honour that you are doing me by making me this proposal but I must beg leave to refuse you.'

John shrugged. 'As you wish. There are as many fish in the sea as ever came out of it.'

'There is no fish as big as this,' I could not refrain from answering.

Thus it was that, in the dead of night, we put together our few goods and chattels and crept forth from the house. John pointed and said: 'My way is eastward. Hetty awaits me.'

I had no way and no one awaited me. But I did not wish to continue with the rogue and so I pointed in the opposite direction and said: 'My way is westward.'

IO

I had no wish to return to my former trade, whether as an employee of Mr Swellington, of John, or some such other middleman, or on my own account. But it was a consolation to me to know that, if honest work were not obtainable, I could always have recourse to work of another, more profitable kind; that whatever misfortune might befall me, I possessed a weapon like to extricate me from it; that, in short, what I carried about with me was more potent than any pistol, more precious than any purse, more efficacious than any elixir.

For many a long day I worked as a labourer, now heaving sacks in Covent Garden and now carting carcases in Smithfield. I slept in many a hovel; under a cart or a bush; on gravestones and kerb-stones. I drank the waters of solitude and found them brackish; I ate the bread of adversity and found it hard. What is a man profited if he shall gain his soul and lose the whole world? The consciousness of my own virtue was little recompense for the consciousness of my hunger, weariness and cold. Honest poverty is no less degrading than dishonest affluence; and the wretches who panted and sweated along beside me seemed far more piteous than any of Mr Swellington's 'irregulars'.

One evening, after the foreman of the gang in which I had been labouring chided me for not working with sufficient ardour (in truth, I was but late recovered from a fever that had turned my bones to water), I resolved that a life of easy virtue was preferable to a virtue that came so hard and I set off for the Shepherd Market, where I knew from of old that such a trade as my former one was plied with vigour. But for lack of a glass in the hovel in which I had been sleeping hugger-mugger with six or seven other wretches, male and female, I had no idea of my present appearance: my locks all dishevelled and tangled; my face covered in bristles; my fingernails broken and grimed; my clothes filthy and threadbare; my shoes so cracked that one big-toe was visible for all the world to see. At the Market a number of elegant ladies and a number of youths no less elegant were walking up and down or loitering in conversation. They looked askance at one so villainous-seeming as myself, two or three of the youths even fluttering and twittering together like birds when a tom approaches. One hussy eventually boarded me and, having eyed me up and down, queried of me in the most disdainful drawl imaginable 'What do you at the meat-rack?'

'The meat-rack, madam?' I asked, not comprehending her drift.

'The customers here,' she went on, 'care for only the finest cuts. I should advise you to make your way to Spitalfields, Blackfriars or some other market less salubrious.'

Slowly it was born in on me, as coach after coach carried away its purchases, as chair after chair inspected the wares on show, that every eye was too much repelled by the filth of my person and the disorder of my dress to be able to observe the quality that was now my sole recommendation. The night proceeded apace; only a few tainted pieces of meat remained on display on the meat-rack; and no one had so much as examined me with care, let alone made any offer. As dawn broke, a drunkard, accoutred in a jacket covered in spew and wine, staggered up to me and made me a proposal that, even in my then state of dejection, I could not accept. At that, he cursed me and wandered off still muttering many an imprecation. Next, a child, wizened and pallid, crept forth from an upturned box and begged some charity from me to fill her stomach;

and all reckless, I gave her the sole coin that I had in my pocket. She told me that the recompense that she had lately earned from some grandee had been snatched from her by a sneak-thief.

When morning had broken, I was standing before a pastry-cook's, peering in through the panes as the servants from the mansions round about ran with their baskets for their masters' and mistresses' breakfast rolls and loaves. All at once a foppish voice was asking me: 'Are you hungry, boy?' (I had noticed how, as my appearance had deteriorated, so had the manner in which others addressed me.) I shook my head in answer to this question, my pride forbidding me to admit the straits in which I found myself. ' 'Tis easy to see that the animal has not fed well for many a long day. Its sides are so fallen in that one may count every bone.' The owner of the voice, a young man with sleeked-down hair and a scent of perfume as overpowering as the stink of honest toil that I carried around with me, was quizzing me through his glass. 'Do you wish to have fodder provided for you in my master's house this evening?'

'I do not know your master.'

'Nor he you. But the Lord – I mean, the Lord, my master – will provide nonetheless.'

'Good sir, I know not what jape or prank this is.'

'No jape, no prank. None in the world! All that my master desires is that you should come to his house and eat the repast provided for you.'

'Your master would seem to be a true Christian gentleman.'

'Of that I know not. But the repast will be good; and for the labour of eating it, you will be rewarded with a guinea.'

'A guinea!'

'A gold guinea. Well, do you consent?'

'What can I do but consent? To such as I a guinea has the potency of a King's command.'

'Good.' Most languidly, a handkerchief raised from time

to time to his nostrils, the young blood gave me directions as to time and place, concluding: 'There is but one small condition. But it is so small that 'twere best if I were to acquaint you with it this evening and not now.' He then reached into his pocket and produced a coin: 'Here, my man! Take this, as an earnest of my master's good intentions. 'Twill buy you one of those loaves at which you were gazing with so much envy. But do not eat too much!' At that, he went about his business.

When evening came, having washed myself as best I could at the pump at Marble Arch, I made my way to the mansion at the time appointed and rang at the bell. The footman seemed not at all surprised to see me, dirty and dishevelled though I was despite all my ablutions, and at once conducted me, as though forewarned of my coming, into an ante-room. Soon the young fop bustled in. 'I am ill dressed for such a mansion as this,' I commenced to excuse myself but he waved my apologies aside with a flutter of his perfumed handkerchief, saying 'My master likes the needy to look needy. You are hungry?' I nodded. 'Good! I feared, when I gave you that coin, that you might take the edge off your appetite. A banquet has been prepared for you.'

Overwhelmed by so much kindness, I knew not what to answer and hung my head. At which the fop continued: 'I spoke of one small condition.'

I nodded. 'Pray apprise me of it.'

'I shall do so; and having done so, I wish to hear no why and wherefore. Are we agreed?'

Again I nodded.

'You will find that the repast will prove an ample and delicious one.' He looked me up and down with some contempt and added: 'I doubt if you will ever have eaten so well in the past; or that you will ever eat so well again in the future. But whatever dish is set before you, it will be your duty to complain.'

'To complain?'

'To complain. That is what I have said. You must send

162

away the consommé for being too hot or too cold; the entrée for being too salt or not salt enough; the roast for – well, I must leave the rest to your native wit, such as it is. Do you understand me?' He was speaking to me as to a child.

'Perfectly,' I retorted, somewhat nettled, even though a number of questions, such as he had expressly forbidden, had risen to my lips.

'You will also complain about the wines, even though they are of the finest vintages that France and Germany can boast. You have followed me?'

'Indeed, sir.'

'Good. Then let us proceed to the dining-room.'

We climbed a vast flight of stairs, lined by many a flunkey, and then entered a hall of prodigious length, with a table, fit to seat a company of forty or fifty, down its centre. A single place was laid, though the whole table was a-glitter with candelabra and every chandelier was ablaze.

'I am to eat alone?'

'Alone. Pray be seated.' In peremptory fashion he flicked the scented handkerchief in the direction of the chair. Somewhat fearful, I went and placed myself in it.

'You will not eat with me?'

'I?' The notion obviously scandalized him. 'Indeed, no! I shall eat in my own time – and place!' He made his way over to the door. 'Now remember my instructions! Please pay heed to them in every particular! Eat and drink nothing until you have first complained about it and it has been replaced!'

He left me and I sat for a while in bewilderment and fear. Then a door, inset in the wall in such a manner that I had not observed it, opened up behind me and a maidservant, a middle-aged, stout party in apron and mob-cap, bustled in with a tureen of steaming soup. 'Good evening, good sir,' she greeted me. 'I trust your appetite is sharp.'

'Thank you, yes,' I answered; and at that she ladled me out a portion and set it down before me in a bowl of the finest porcelain with a gold spoon beside it. I tasted it, the maidservant looking on with some anxiety, and indeed it was delicious, being some concoction of chicken-stock, peas and savoury herbs; but I remembered my instructions, wrinkled up my nose, all but spat what was in my mouth into my spoon and said: ' 'Tis oversalted! I cannot drink such stuff for fear of puking!'

At that the good woman snatched away the plate, saying, all tremulous: 'Please forgive me, kind sir! Wait but a moment! Have patience! I shall remedy the defect!'

Another tureen was brought (or perhaps it was but the same tureen) and again the soup was served. It tasted as delicious as ever and this time I drank it without complaint.

The maidservant now, with still trembling hand, poured some wine into a goblet and handed it to me to taste. ' 'Tis the finest Bordeaux wine,' she explained.

I sipped, and again remembering my instructions, I then cried out: 'This wine has not come from Bordeaux, good madam! Do not tell me such falsehoods! It is but the foul lees of that butt of malmsey in which the Duke of Clarence met his end!'

'Oh, sir! Good, sir! You must forgive me! One moment! Let me repair the defect!' The good woman was so agitated that I pitied her from all my heart, even though I must needs proceed with the comedy for the sake of that guinea.

I sniffed at a chicken and declared that it had been hung too long and then sniffed at a partridge and said that it had not been hung long enough; I spat out a piece of the tenderest beef imaginable and declared that it was so tough that I should choke on it; I ranted that a pigeon-pie was all bones and a pork-cutlet all gristle; I shouted (the comedy by now taking a hold on me) that I had never eaten so villainous a meal in all my born days or drunk wine that approached so near to vinegar and even worse. Soon the good woman was as agitated as with the Dance of St Vitus, the sweat running down, mingled with tears, over her homely cheeks and chin and her voice all a-sob, with, 'Pray forgive me, good sir!', 'Do not chastise me so hard, dear sir, though I deserve it, the Good Lord knows!', 'I am a fond, foolish woman!' and things of like kind.

When she produced a sorbet, a triumph of the culinary art, I sent the dish spinning across the table with: 'How dare you serve me with such pig's-swill as this!' Weeping loudly now, the serving-woman hurried from the dining-room, clutching the sorbet to her ample bosom.

I waited for her return; until at last I heard the door open behind me. I looked round. 'Enough of this farce!' said a deep voice; and there was the serving-woman, her mob-cap removed to reveal a bald pate and her bodice unfastened to reveal two hairy paps. 'I have spilled in the kitchen,' the voice went on.

I rose to my feet, guessing (rightly) that this must be the master of the house, who had played this prank on me.

'Begone!' he shouted, as he might to any cur that had strayed in from the street. 'My major domo will see you at the door.' He pointed, not to the door through which I had entered, but at that to the kitchen. 'Pray take the back stairs!'

At the bottom of the stairs, the young fop was waiting. 'I trust you ate well?' he smirked, handing me a golden guinea delicately between forefinger and thumb. 'My master was little pleased with you at first but you warmed to the work.'

'I do not comprehend –' I began to stammer; but he cut me short, with: 'No whys or wherefores! A good night to you!'

As I walked out into the yard, he slammed the door behind me as though to say, 'Good riddance to bad rubbish!'

Thus again furnished with money, I was able to make some purchases of clothes of a modest nature, to visit the barber and to have the cobbler repair my shoes. This done, I repaired to the meat-rack, where, in a trice, a lady drew up in her carriage and four, quizzed me for a moment and then invited me to climb up and join her.

My fortunes seemed at last to have undergone a change; but what was my chagrin and despair when, bedded with the most luscious of beauties on a bed of the softest down, I found that, for all my earnest endeavours, my manhood remained no less soft than the mattress. Gentle reader, if you be of the male sex, you will no doubt be able to sympathize with me in my plight; if, on the other hand, you be of the other sex, then you will no doubt be able to appreciate the fury of she who had been but lately paying me the most extravagant compliments. 'But give me time, madam,' I pleaded; to which she shrilled at me: 'Give *you* time! No man has made such a request of me ever in my whole life! It is I who must ask them to give *me* time!'

Praying that mine was but a temporary indisposition, I left her house in utter ignominy, to return to the meat-rack, where again a carriage halted before me and the most melodious voice in the world called me over. But this voice became as grating as any corn-crake's when once again I could not rise to the occasion. No doubt because of the nervosity that I suffered as a result of these encounters, the indisposition that I had supposed to be temporary now seemed permanent; for, reversing what is usual among the male sex, I now found that the mere thought of a woman could inflate my ardour but her actual presence at once deflated it again. So it was that now for a second time my fortunes were a-droop, as sadly as my manhood in the chambers from which I was expelled with so much fury. The lot of a fallen man is, indeed, far harder than that of a fallen woman. She may simulate, with many a sigh, groan, moan and wriggle an ecstasy she does not feel; but if the man's ecstasy may not be felt by his partner, then there is nought that he may do to simulate it.

Like some knight of old whose sword had buckled in his grasp, I no longer had the wherewithal to defend myself against a world grown hostile to me. How I was saved from this lamentable predicament will be the subject of my next chapter.

I I

I called at the same information office at which I had first
encountered Mr Swellington, in the hope of finding some
employment that would make no demands of my still
depleted resources, and there renewed acquaintance with
the dame, dressed all in black bombazine, who sat at the
receipt of custom among her rolls and ledgers. She quizzed
me through the glass that hung on a pinckbeck chain
round her neck and then enquired if I were not the young
gentleman who had been engaged by Mrs Swellington but
a few months back. I assented to the truth of this; at which
she told me that she had tried in vain to find some replace-
ment for me for Mrs Swellington's establishment; that the
poor lady was in a desperate and distracted state, with a
staff inadequate to the number and importunities of her
customers; and that, without a doubt, if I were to wish to
resume my former position, Mrs Swellington would be
willing to let bygones be bygones and take me back into
her protection.

I replied that nothing would induce me to return; at
which the beldame sighed, pursed her lips and said that,
to be candid with me, this answer did not surprise her.
Mrs Swellington, though a woman of quality, was noted
for her lack of consideration for the well-being of her
servants. 'There is,' she went on, 'another lady in the same
way of business, who is also on my books. Her name is
Mrs Sheldrake and, though her establishment is smaller
and her trade more modest, she uses those that serve her
with a greater generosity. She was in here but yesterday
morning, with the request that I should look out for a
fine, upstanding young man, such as yourself.'

'Madam,' I replied, 'I no longer wish the kind of employment that you have mind in for me, however generous the lady of the house.'

She again quizzed me through the glass, with such amazement and then asked: 'How so? I do not comprehend you.'

Too much ashamed to reveal my shortcoming, I sought for a pretext: 'While working for Mrs Swellington, I learned the errors of my ways. I wish now for an honest life, so that I may eventually prove myself worthy of the love of a good woman.'

'An honest life and a good woman are both hard to find in this metropolis,' she retorted, shaking her head. 'They are particularly hard to find if you wish also to find a livelihood.'

'There must be honest toil a-plenty in a city such as this.'

'There is certainly honest slavery a-plenty,' she replied. 'Of honest toil I know not.' She drew a ledger towards her and then, after some deliberation, told me an address, hard by Pall Mall, where a certain lady was in need of a footman. I was to go in my the back entrance, where a Mrs Stoop, the housekeeper, would look me over. At that, the good woman again shook her head, murmuring that it was sad to see a man so waste his natural ability, and bade me adieu and God speed.

I had but entered the rear door of a vast, gloomy mansion and introduced myself to this Mrs Stoop, a sour spindle-shanks who seemed to be attempting to read my character not in my face but elsewhere, when to my horror the mistress of the house appeared on the scene and was revealed to be one of the lickerish, open-mouthed dames who had been responsible for reducing me to my present crest-fallen state. I dissimulated any knowledge of her, and she did likewise in respect to myself, even though her previously grouchy expression had vanished as soon as she set eyes on me. 'And who may this be, Mrs Stoop?' she asked, fanning herself so vigorously that the powder blew off her in flakes.

' 'Tis a recruit for footman, an't please Your Ladyship,' returned Mrs Stoop. 'He has but this moment arrived from the information office and I am in the way of sounding his character.'

'Let me have a word with him, good Mrs Stoop. You may see to the linen-press.'

'But I saw to it, an't please Your Ladyship, but an hour agone.'

'Then you may see to the preserve cupboard,' the mistress commanded; and at that she turned to me and invited me with an imperious condescension most unlike her manner to me at Mr Swellington's: 'Pray come up, my man.'

Once we were in her chamber, however, she threw all modesty to the winds, crying out, her arms flung about me: 'Danny, dear Danny! I and many another have sent up and down the town in search of you. 'Twas said that some lady not far distant from the palace – indeed the Monarch's very sister – had secreted you in a lodging, where she visited you daily. Is't true?'

'No, indeed, madam,' I replied, attempting to extricate myself from her embraces, which were growing increasingly indiscreet. 'I left Mrs Swellington for employment more honest.'

' 'Tis true, she is a right cheating jade. But you have no need, dear Danny, of such or indeed any intermediary. I can provide you with all the employment that you may desire through my friends and acquaintances.'

'You are very kind, madam,' I replied, mightily embarrassed. 'But for the moment the state of my health prevents me from such employment as you have in mind.'

Greatly alarmed, she at once desisted from handling me. 'I trust you have not the pox or the clap?'

'Oh, indeed no, madam! 'Tis merely some species of rheum that makes my head heavy, so that I have the greatest difficulty in rising. 'Twill pass, I do not doubt.'

'But if you have difficulty in rising, how will you serve as footman?'

169

'I can promise in no wise to shirk my duties.'

For a moment she pondered; then she shook her head, her fan all a-flutter. 'I am grieved, Danny, but I cannot have such as you in so humble a position as my footman, after you have enjoyed the freedom of every limb of my body.'

'But I should not presume, my lady, on our previous intimacy!'

'Besides, you are too refined for the coarse tasks that I might require of you. You are too much the gentleman, Danny dear. But stay a moment!' At this, she went to a secretaire, drew out a purse and inserted a hand in it, saying: 'Here, Danny, is a little *douceur* for old times' sake.' She then extended to me a sovereign, which, minding me of the parlous state of my finances, I needs must accept, even though my pride urged me not to do so. 'As soon as your rheum has dissipated, pray be sure to get in touch with me. I have no doubt that I can then put you in the way of no lack of highly paid employment.'

Having thanked her most graciously, my hand on my heart, I begged to take my leave; at which: 'Ah, Danny, Danny, Danny!' she cried out in an access of adoration, throwing her arms again around me. 'Never have I seen a better turned pair of ankles than yours.'

'Madam, you are too kind.'

Greatly disconsolate, I was making my way down Pall Mall when all on a sudden I heard a voice summon me, as though I were some porter, to come and lend a hand. A group of fellows were descending the stairs of a gaming-house, supporting between them what I first assumed to be one far gone in drink. It was only when I approached them that I realized that their burden was, in fact, a gentleman wholly sober who had lost, I then knew not how, the use of his nether limbs. He was a man of Apollonian beauty, not far below my own, with the most agreeable voice imaginable, even though he was at the moment shouting: 'Careful, damn you! Do you wish to tip me into the gutter?' His servants, all elderly or weaklings, were evidently much afraid of him.

'Allow me, sir,' I said, taking him from them as though he were a baby and carrying him, in my two arms, down the steps and into his waiting carriage.

'Thank you, sirrah,' he said, fumbling in his pocket for a coin. Then he looked up and, obviously liking what he saw, remarked: ' 'Tis evident that you are a man not merely of strength but also of parts. May I ask your name?'

'Danny Hill, sir.'

'I have heard something of you, Mr Hill, but what and where and how I cannot now remember. I also once knew a certain Miss Fanny Hill. I am Lord Chatterley.'

'I have, of course, heard of you, Your Lordship.'

' 'Twould be surprising if you had not.'

'Your fame has gone abroad. As, indeed, has that of your lady.'

'Pray mount, if you have nothing better to do. Since I received my wound in the Lowlands, there are few manly pleasures left to me. I am on my way from losing money at the tables to spending money on buying a necklace for Her Ladyship. You may assist me in my choice.'

Thus it came about that I became first an acquaintance and then a friend of the famous Lord Chatterley. At the time of our first encounter, his lady was in distant Derbyshire, having conceived an aversion for the polite society of the town and a positive passion for the uncouth society of the country. She, who had once been present nightly at plays, balls and routs, dancing on until dawn was breaking over the Thames, was now never to be seen in St James's, devoting herself (as Lord Chatterley informed me) to the solo care of her humble cottagers, for whom she had started a little school, where she herself acted as mistress to such of them as she felt might benefit from her evening classes. Her discipline was strict (again as Lord Chatterley informed me) but her heart was large. Not unnaturally I was eager to meet this paragon; so that, when Lord Chatterley informed me that he was seeking just such an attendant as myself, strong enough to carry him, educated enough to amuse him and handsome enough to please him, I was easily persuaded to accept the employment and to travel with him to Derbyshire, where he owned a vast estate.

Lady Chatterley was certainly beautiful, even if her limbs were, if possible, too well made, since their plump fullness was rather to the prejudice of that delicate slimness required by the nicer judges of beauty. Her eyes were black and ardent and nothing could have been prettier than her mouth and lips, which, soft and full, closed over a range of the evenest and whitest teeth. But to my dismay she seemed, like Lady Gloria, to be wholly indifferent to my charms and even to resent my presence at the side of her husband. This poor husband, who palpably adored her, loading her with costly presents, she treated with a marked haughtiness and disdain.

'I fear that Her Ladyship does not care greatly for me,' I said to Lord Chatterley in the privacy of his chamber, after one of those occasions when she had been markedly chilly to me. Although I had been but two days in the house, he had already given orders that only I must dress and undress him, bathe him and shave him.

'Think nothing of it. Such is the beauty of her character – a beauty on a par with the beauty of her person – that she must reserve the greater part of her love for the poor, the uneducated and the oppressed. You, who are handsome and well educated and will no doubt one day be the possessor of a fortune, have no need of her love and therefore she does not accord it to you. She is a truly rare and remarkable person.'

But I had already noticed (what he, because of his disability, had little opportunity to do) that this truly rare and remarkable person reserved her love for the poor, the uneducated and the oppressed only of one sex. Many was the time when I had heard her shrilly upbraiding one of the serving-maids for some trivial misdemeanour; many the time that I had witnessed her kick or strike out at these same serving-maids with the vigour and malice of any ill-tempered slut in the stews; many the time that I came on Molly, Doris, Mary or Jane in a flood of tears after Her Ladyship had been particularly censorious and spleenish. Lord Chatterley had already told me that Her Ladyship, for all her connections with half the noble houses of England and France, was one who believed that, in the eyes of our Maker, all of us were equal; and I can therefore only believe that she imagined that her Maker's eye was not on her when she bade poor fifteen-year-old Molly maintain vigil till the early hours so that the girl could bring her a tisane to allay a possible fit of wakefulness; or when she kept poor fifty-year-old Doris out in a tempest as she changed one pair of shoes for another at leisurely pace in the shelter of her carriage.

As I have related, Lord Chatterley had already told me of Her Ladyship's little school. One evening, as I was passing down a corridor to join His Lordship in the library, I heard from behind a closed door the voice of one repeating laboriously, in the rude accents of that benighted part of these islands: 'The cut sut on the mut' (or so, indeed, it sounded); at which I then heard Her Ladyship correct in the mildest and most winsome manner imaginable, quite unlike that tone that she used to correct her serving-women: 'No, no, Mr Mellors. You must say "The cat – sat – on the – mat." ' Consumed with an unquenchable curiosity, I knelt to the keyhole and applied my eye. Here was no class, such as His Lordship had led me to imagine, but merely a single pupil, a heavy and hunched hulk of a man, his porcine visage covered with whiskers and his finger-nails so black that it would have been possible to grow potatoes beneath them. Leaning over him at a desk of the kind common in a village schoolroom was Lady Chatterley, a cane in her hand and sweetest of smiles on her face. 'Again,' she bade him; and again, with not the smallest difference, he repeated in his gruff, rumbling voice, 'The cut sut on the mut.' Her Ladyship flexed the cane in her hand, still smiling sweetly, and said 'Come, come, Mr Mellors! You would not wish to be so bad a pupil that I must needs apply some medicine to your posterior.'

I could not observe how this diverting scene then ended, since I heard footsteps approaching and hurriedly arose from my semi-recumbent posture before the butler (for it was he) could discover me. As we came face to face, I enquired in casual manner: 'Tell me, Mr Tulliver, who is this Mr Mellors of whom I have heard tell?'

Mr Tulliver, a very proper gentleman, who had spent many years in the service of the Chatterleys, shook his head, tut-tutted and murmured something about 'below-stairs gossip'. Then he went on, 'Mr Mellors, like his father and his grandfather before him, is head game-keeper. Unlike them, he is mighty eager to improve himself and to this end Her Ladyship has interested herself in his case.' At that, he strode on; but 'twas already clear to me that, though Mr Mellors might himself have laid many a snare and prepared many a mantrap, he was unlike to escape from the toils that Her Ladyship had devised for him.

Wearied of carrying His Lordship hither and yon, whether by myself or with the assistance of some other of the men, I hit on the idea, having seen the old gardener pushing a wheelbarrow through the garden, on devising some similar means of propulsion. I laboured long on the construction of what was, in effect, a kind of go-cart; and laboured yet longer to persuade His Lordship that it was not beneath his dignity to ride in it. Lady Chatterley made great mock both of him and of me, saying that he looked like a great baby, travelling in a fashion so mean, and that I looked like some French navvy, pushing such a burden before me. But once he grew accustomed to this method of locomotion, His Lordship was delighted, rewarding me with a splendid gold watch, a diamond of great price and other such demonstrations of his gratitude and affection. This also Her Ladyship took mighty amiss, getting her revenge by bidding me in peremptory fashion to do this or that task for her as though I were some menial. She was right to be angry with me for the cart, for (though such was not my intention when I constructed it) it was to prove her undoing.

One balmy day, after His Lordship and I had spent many an hour in the study together elucidating one of Mr Pope's more philosophical and less satirical masterworks, we decided that, since, as another poet has it, *dulce est desipere in loco*, we should take a turn through the grounds. Led wholly by chance (for, though I had heard a certain prattle below stairs, I had of course paid no need to it), I pushed His Lordship down some narrow paths, odorous with the smell of the lavender-bushes that bordered them, and so towards a little belvedere that stood, half-ruined, in a dell. His Lordship, being in the best humours, was full of my praises, remarking on the beauty of my voice as I had read out Mr Pope's couplets to him, on the freshness of my complexion now that it had benefited from the country air and on the amplitude of my muscles as I pushed him ahead of me.

All at once, the sound of womanish laughter came to our ears, succeeded by laughter that was obviously male. His Lordship started and looked at me in wild surmise. I put my finger to my lips and pushed him faster, my curiosity to discover what was taking place in the belvedere surmounting my natural modesty. There was a crack at one side, where the lath had mouldered away (I had chanced to notice this crack only the day before during a solitary walk) and through this we could observe everything without ourselves being observed. The door of the belvedere had partly fallen in and its floor was now covered with grass, making a bed for (my hand trembles even now as I write it) – Mr Mellors and Her Ladyship! Seeing the pair, His Lordship let out an oath but I enjoined him to silence by quickly placing a hand on his lips (an act that he fortunately did not regard as insubordination or take in any way amiss). Mr Mellors was already unbuttoned and the engine of his love-assault filled me with both amaze and envy, since it did not fall

175

far short of my own in length and girth. Her Ladyship's ample bosoms were bare and rising in the warmest throbs; but even their pride, whiteness and pleasing resistance to the touch could not bribe Mr Mellors's restless and still grimy hands from roving; so that, petticoats and shift taken up, he was soon at pains to open up a way for the main attack.

As his prodigious stiffness drove forward with fury, His Lordship was evidently as rapt as I at the spectacle of the game-keeper's ardour, matched by an ardour no less in the partner of his pleasure. Lost to everything but the enjoyment of her favourite feelings (certainly lost to all modesty and shame), the strammel was now retorting his thrusts with a concert of springy heaves, keeping time exactly with the most pathetic sighs, whilst her limbs kept wreathing and intertwisting with his in convulsive folds. Soon she was crying out in the ravings of her pleasure-frenzy, 'Oh Sir! . . . Good sir! . . . Pray do not spare me!' It was at that moment (as I later recollected it though I was then unaware) that His Lordship, overcome by the emotions rampaging within his breast, put out his hand to me; but such were the emotions rampaging within my own breast as well, that that hand might as well have been my own. All her accents now faltering into heart-fetched sighs, she closed her eyes in the sweet death at that instant when the balsamic injection interfused her; and a second later I realized (with what pleasure can be imagined) that I had, in a trice, been cured of my disability.

His Lordship and I stayed on to watch as the minx and her poltroon now exchanged a quantity of mixed chat, frolic and childish humour, their clothes still all awry and their faces red and sweat-streaked from so much exertion. Never have I witnessed such an absurd display of love-delights, turtle-billing, toying, kissing, chucking and philandering of every kind. At one point, Her Ladyship wandered out from the belvedere and began to pick some *Bellis perennis* (known to the crude country-folk of those parts as *daisies*), which she then must needs weave into a chain, to place about the neck of Mr Mellors's engine; Mr Mellors, poor dolt, being as delighted with this necklet as though it were made of rubies. Later, she plucks a blade of grass and first uses it to tickle his point of all delight and then (he much wriggling) actually inserts it. But when she begins to withdraw the grass, he bellows like any bull, telling her, ' 'Tis sword-grass, Your Ladyship! Have a care! 'Tis sword-grass!'

At that, His Lordship and I beat our retreat: he less angered by what he had discovered than I had supposed and using me with an even greater kindness; and I greatly relieved that what I had for so long lost had now been restored to me.

Whether it was because of his discovery of his dear wife's treachery or whether it was that, like many another, he had found in me something irresistible, His Lordship now showered me with even more gifts and compliments, was even more insistent that I should never leave his side and, in short, behaved to me as though he were to me father, brother and comrade all combined. At first, some of his attentions were not wholly welcome to me, but I reasoned thus with myself: Here was one who had given what many a man holds dearer even than life while fighting for his country; if a man is blind, who would not lend him the use of his eyes, and if a man is halt, who would not lend him the use of his legs?; and, when all was said and done, what passed between us did no hurt to me and gave some pleasure to him. Many was the time that we went together to the belvedere to watch Her Ladyship and her love at their sport, like any Titania with her Bottom; and many was the time that, once more back in London, we repaired to some such establishment as Mr Swellington's (though not to his) to our mutual satisfaction, His Lordship assisting as my cannoneer while I fired off salvo on salvo. It was thus that envious gossips and scandal-mongers came to speak of me as 'Lord Chatterley's Lover', even though the estimable emotions that I had for him were purely those of Friendship, and Love I could feel for none other than my beloved Lucy.

Now I must come to the tale of how I found my dear mother once again. Lord and Lady Chatterley had been invited to Castle ———, the place of my birth, though then I did not know this, for the nuptials of the deceased Duke's supposed daughter, a comely and saucy girl a year younger than myself. Lady Chatterley, who had become increasingly reluctant to leave her Mr Mellors, be it only for a sojourn of a week, told His Lordship that he must needs visit the Castle without her, giving as her pretexts that the noble pile was as cold as any iceberg; that she liked the Duchess indifferent well; and that the fare served up was such as to make her puke. The truth was (as I learned from the gossip below stairs) far different: Mr Mellors had been under suspicion of courting Molly; at which Her Ladyship had despatched the wretched girl to another post at the other end of the country, and, fearful of some similar recurrence, had resolved never to let her game-keeper gallant out of her sight until she tired of him. It needs no saying that Lord Chatterley, in turn, would not let me out of his sight, informing Her Grace that he would be bringing with him his 'nephew'. Since neither my master nor my mistress had either brother nor sister, Her Grace no doubt knew this to be a falsehood; but she valued Lord Chatterley, as indeed did all who knew him, and was therefore prepared to be complaisant.

The daughter, one Phoebe, was greatly taken with me and, it soon became apparent to me, was more interested in finding her way to my bed that very evening than to the church on the morrow. She sought out occasion to converse with me alone and, in the boldest manner, informed me of her wishes. On my protesting that I could not break into the orchard ere ever her husband-to-be (a pestilential ninny) had tasted of its fruits, she replied that a little dillying and dallying outside the orchard gates could do no one any harm. Greatly reluctant, I then agreed to wait for her in my chamber after we had all retired to bed.

Since the night was uncommonly warm and so as to make as much speed as possible in a business that filled me with as much apprehension as excitation, I diverted myself of all my garments and then threw a robe of finest silk, a present from Lord Chatterley, over my ardent nakedness. Many a minute passed and I had decided that the cheating jade either could not or would not come when I heard a gentle tapping at the door of my chamber. I rushed to it and pulled it open, only to discover, not the beauteous eighteen-year-old, but a dame already past her summer. She placed a finger on her lips and slipped into the room. 'Pray forgive me this intrusion, kind sir, but the Lady Phoebe has begged me to come to you. For tonight, whether because she has surmised that somewhat is afoot or whether because she would in any event wish to take all precaution, Her Grace has decided to sleep in the Lady Phoebe's chamber. There is no way that the Lady Phoebe may come to you this night; but she hopes that ere long she will be able to continue that conversation that she began with you with so much pleasure.'

I made some gesture of annoyance, turning away from the dame; and as I did so, my robe inadvertently fell open. Whereupon she let out a shriek so terrifying that one might have supposed that she had discovered me to have a tail and cloven hooves. 'What is amiss, my good woman?' I asked her.

'Oh, sir, please, sir –!' She was gawping and pointing. 'I have only seen one such before in my whole life and I could not mistake its exact replica in every detail. Forgive me, sir – but who was your father?'

'Alas, I know not. Nor do I know who was my mother. Good folk, living not far from here, brought me up as though I were their son.'

At that, much to my amaze, the woman threw her arms around me. ' 'Tis my Danny!' she cried out in an access of joy, the tears beginning to course down her cheeks. 'I should have known it anywhere.' And then she began to pour out the whole story that I have already related,

179

revealing to me that if, on the one side, my parentage was indeed base, on the other it was the highest imaginable.

When she had completed her account, I bethought me of the effect that it might have, if revealed, on Lord Chatterley and others with whom I had become acquainted through his good offices. I therefore took her hand in mine and said to her: 'Mother – if I may indeed call you Mother now for the first time – the story that you have told me must, for the sake of my father, remain forever a secret between us. I am no Papist; but I should not wish to bring disgrace, humiliation and shame on the Supreme Pontiff.'

The good woman inclined her head: 'Oh, Danny, that was certainly not my wish.'

'I am heartily glad to have made your acquaintance after all these years; and I can promise you that, if my patron, Lord Chatterley, continues to use me well, then you shall want for nothing.'

'You are too good!' And at that, quite overcome, the good woman needs must seize my hand and cover it with kisses.

Thus mother and son were reunited in the selfsame place where they had first come together. The next day, when the nuptials were over I must needs make my departure and I had no way to find my mother or the Lady Phoebe again, try though I might. But to each I sent secretly on our return to London; to my mother a goodly sum of money; to the Lady Phoebe a letter protesting my disappointment and my continuing infatuation and my hope to be joined with her before too long. In writing this last I was, I must confess, guilty of deception: in truth I had no desire to be joined with one whom I had now guessed to be my half-sister.

12

Though it was of course in no way my intention to do so, it was I who, in a sense, brought about the death of my benefactor. We had gone out to the belvedere, I pushing him in his little cart, with the object of enjoying our usual sport, unbeknown to Her Ladyship and Mr Mellors, when all on a sudden the skies had opened with the same vehemence as the gallant game-keeper, and we outside the belvedere had been inundated at precisely the same moment as Her Ladyship within it. I was eager to hurry His Lordship to shelter: but such was His Lordship's then state of enthusiasm that he over-rode me. Thus it was that he contracted a rheum, that became a fever, that became a congestion of the lungs.

At the thought of the death of this man who had been my patron and benefactor, I was – need I record? – quite unmanned, going down on my knees at his bedside, clasping his hand in mine, and begging him, with many a tear, not to leave me to a life of destitution. He put out his other hand, to pat my head or stroke my cheek as I supposed; but the hand descended lower, as he bade me a last farewell. 'Do not fear, Danny,' he consoled me. 'For the happiness that you have brought me, I have already secured your happiness for the rest of your days.'

I could not but feel a leap of joy within me as I learned of this generosity; then this hand fell from me, his head dropped back on his pillow and I knew that all was over.

After the funeral, having been apprised by the lawyer that the good man had indeed done all that he had promised me, dividing his estates between myself and that wanton who had been his wife, I set off to find my Lucy, not knowing what I should learn of her. It was possible that she had consented to be betrothed to someone other, in her despair at ever again being united with myself; it was possible that she had immured herself in some order of religious sisters, preferring a life of solitary barrenness to one of fruitfulness in arms other than my own; it was even possible (dreadful thought!) that, having been deprived of any reason for prolonging her existence, she had wasted away like a woodland flower wrenched from its proper soil.

If she were still alive and if she were still single, my felicity was, even so, not incontestably assured. Her father might remember the ill-bred hobbledehoy (for so he had called me) who had held clandestine converse with his daughter on a number of occasions. I also knew that, enraged by the division of Lord Chatterley's estates, Her Ladyship had been breathing, not merely fire, but also most noxious poisons againt me, confiding to all and sundry, over the funeral breakfast and even over the coffin itself, that I had won over her dear, good husband with the most abominable practices; that I had precipitated his decline by trundling him about the garden at the height of a storm; that I had then hastened his demise by the importunities of my demands on him; and that I was well-known in London as person of neither morals nor principles, who had for long lived by the sale of a commodity that a true gentleman would be as little willing to offer up for barter as his immortal soul. Those who had previously been looking askance at Mr Mellors, newly appointed steward of the household and decked out in the most absurd and ill-fitting mourning taken from his dead master's presses, now began to look askance at me. I fear that as a result few of those present returned home in contemplation of the virtues of the deceased, preferring instead to ruminate on the vices, both imagined and real, of his relicts.

All these doubts tormented me on the long journey by coach from the one end of England to the other, my mind as much buffeted by anxiety as my body by the irregularities of the high road. To own one of the largest fortunes in the country would prove a meagre compensation if I could not also count Lucy among my possessions. But what if she were married, enclosed or passed from this mortal world? What if her father, a man of old-fashioned principles and ancient lineage, were to refuse her hand to one who, though rich, might appear in his eyes an upstart? Gossip travels on the wind like gossamer; and some might already have reached his domain.

I put up at a neighbouring inn and at once made enquiry. What was my joy to learn from the honest innkeeper that my Lucy was, indeed, still alive and unmarried and that she was in residence at the manor with her elderly father, her mother having now deceased. The good man then shook his head and went on, to my dismay: 'But you will find things sadly changed up at the big house.'

'How so?' I queried.

'You will see for yourself, good sir,' he rejoined. 'I am not one to gossip, as many folk will do in these parts. You will see in due course.' My curiosity and his greed both being insatiable, a coin at once elicited from him the intelligence that, after the death of his lady, the squire had been driven by grief to the gambling tables of every capital of Europe, with his daughter in train; that he has lost all his fortune and that his mansion was now mortgaged to the hilt; and that, if he could not soon find the necessary funds, the Jews would ruin him. Sad at heart for my poor Lucy, reduced to such an unwonted state of destitution, but hopeful of my ability to rescue her, I set off almost at once for the house, resolving that I should not remind the old man, her father, that Lucy and I had ever had conversation together and persuaded that she herself would no doubt also find it expedient to attempt to keep him in ignorance of my identity.

Such a scene of desolation met my eye as we made our way up a drive overgrown with tares and crowded in on every side with brambles! At the gatehouse, the gate hanging askew on its hinges, none had come forth to ask our business; and indeed it was unlike that anyone still lived there, since the thatch was all fallen in. A famished mongrel bitch ran out to bark at us but, at a crack from my coachman's whip, slunk away into the rampant undergrowth. Many panes of the house were broken and stuffed with paper or rags, the parterres were now all a riot of docks and darnel and, when I pulled at the bell, it came away in my hand. In answer to much repeated knocking, an old crone, gap-toothed, rheumy-eyed and vile-smelling, tottered to the door and, with much gasping and grunting, eased away the bolts to inform me in the most ill-tempered manner imaginable, 'We no longer use this entrance.' On my asking if her master were at home, she left me in a bare, icy hall and, muttering to herself, wandered off into the murky interior of the house. It was indeed as if Prince Charming had come to awaken his Sleeping Beauty!

The squire's wig was all askew, he wore no cravat and his shoes were in urgent need of patching, as was his hose of darning. No doubt supposing me to be one of his creditors, he seemed far from pleased to see me, enquiring of me what was my business in the peremptory manner of one who knows that he is like to be at a disadvantage. I answered him with all the civility and suavity at my disposal, making him a deep bow. I was, I said, but passing through the place and had thought to call on him to bring him news of the death of Lord Chatterley, who had but lately passed away and whom I knew to have been dear to him. At once his whole bearing changed and he begged me to accompany him into the withdrawing-room, where (so he said) a fire was burning.

The fire was smoking, rather than burning, but at least the room contained some chairs, even if the mongrel bitch seemed to have been sitting in each of them in turn. 'Poor Lord Chatterley!' the squire went on. 'A brave soldier and a brave man! I do not doubt but that in the generations ahead his name will still be on many a lip!' He drew forth a grubby handkerchief, as I supposed to dry a tear, but instead he coughed into it, the smoke having evidently entered his lungs. 'I did indeed hear a rumour of his death before you apprised me of it. Am I right in thinking that you are that Mr Danny Hill, his nephew?'

I acknowledged that this indeed was so, a little amazed that he had no recollection of me.

'I have heard much of your great devotion to your uncle; of his affection for you; and of his kindness to you in his testamentary dispositions. May I perhaps offer you a glass of madeira wine?'

In other circumstances honesty might have provoked me to deny any consanguinity with my patron and benefactor; but since Lucy was at stake, I felt no compunction in benefiting from the misapprehension. As though reading my thoughts, the old man now went on: 'I shall ask my daughter, the only solace of my old age and widowerhood, to bring the glasses and the decanter. Our staff here is but small, for since the death of my dear wife I have had no appetite for pomp and show.' He then went out to the stairwell and shouted up it: 'Lucy! Lucy my dear! Come down! Lord Chatterley's nephew is here and we wish for some refreshment.'

No refreshment could have been more intoxicating than the sight of my dearest dear, in no whit changed from that vision of beauty that I had first glimpsed so many moons before. Seeing me, she started, as was natural; reddened; and then paled to alabaster. Fearing lest she might cry out or swoon and so betray us, I put a finger to my lips, at the same time giving her a gaze of joyful complicity.

Excusing the plainness of his daughter's attire (it was indeed such as would more have befitted a maidservant than a lady of her station) the squire repeated yet again that, since his wife's death, all was simplicity in his establishment and mode of living.

He could not have conducted himself towards me with a greater cordiality than he did from that moment onwards and I reproached myself for all my previous doubts and fears. Here was a man who was quick to appreciate merit in another; and it was obvious that both the accidents of birth and calumnies of gossip-mongers were alike matters of indifference to him. If some delicacy persuaded him to maintain the fiction that I was the nephew of Lord Chatterley, then I was prepared to accommodate him.

The invitation to a glass of Madeira became an invitation to dinner; the invitation to dinner an invitation to stay the night; and so, step by step, I soon found myself installed both in his house and his affections.

On my first night in the gloomy mansion, my Lucy, all a-tremble with apprehension and joy, crept secretly down the corridor and into my chamber, her father meantime snoring so loudly that the whole house was reverberant with the din. 'Danny!' she cried. 'At last! I have dreamed so often of this moment!'

'Lucy!' I returned. 'I, too, have dreamed nightly of this moment! Even during the busiest day, your image has rarely been absent from my mind! All that I have striven to do and all that I have succeeded in doing would have been impossible but for your invisible encouragement!' At that our lips met in the sweetest of rapture, her breast pressed to mine. It was when, overcome by the exquisite pleasure of our closeness, she attempted an even greater intimacy that I at last felt obliged to push her away from me. 'Tis said that there is none so prudish as the rake reformed; and my longing to preserve her maiden modesty until the moment of our nuptials was even more potent than my longing to enjoy her there and then. 'Be patient, Lucy!' I bade her. 'Soon, very soon, we shall lie together as man and wife! I should not wish any bride of mine to be other than wholly spotless when she came to me at God's altar.'

'Then you mean to ask my father for my hand?'

I was amazed that she should doubt it. 'Certainly!' I cried. 'What else?'

She hung her head, a blush overmantling the previous flawless white of her cheeks. 'I thought that . . . now that . . .,' she stammered.

'Yes, Lucy dear?' I prompted her.

'You are now one of the richest men in the kingdom. You may choose where you will. The grandest lady in the whole land would be glad to take you for her lord and master.'

'There is no lady grander than you,' I assured her gently.

But still she hung her head. Then she said, in almost a whisper: 'But how am I to leave my beloved father? What is to become of him? I hesitate to tell you this but, crazed from the death of my mother, he has acted imprudently and foolishly and . . . .'

'I know all, Lucy. Have no fears! I shall attend to his debts and he shall never want, as long as it is in my power.'

'Oh, Danny!' She again threw herself in my arms. 'You have made me the happiest woman in the world!'

'You do not doubt that your father will give his consent?'

'Indeed not! How could he fail to accept as son-in-law one so good, decent, proper and rich as yourself?'

So it came about that, after many trials and tribulations and after a great continuous expenditure of my vital forces, I at last came safe to haven with my Lucy. The house of her father, though he invited us to share it with him, seemed to me too poor and simple for one so beauteous and exceptional as the lady who was now Mrs Hill; and so, having given orders for its repairs and having paid off all my father-in-law's debts and made him a handsome allowance, we quitted it for the three mansions left to me by Lord Chatterley. To one of these mansions, I invited my mother to come as housekeeper, at the same time most earnestly enjoining her to continue to maintain the strictest secrecy about the relationship between us, for the sake of my father, my dear, good wife and the children that, I had no doubt, would soon bless our union.

To this same mansion also came, after an interval, Mr Mellors as head game-keeper. Having taught him the rudiments of polite speech and behaviour, together with

187

the necessity of changing his linen and keeping his person correct and clean, Lady Chatterley, wearying of one so rapidly eradicating all that differentiated the two of them from each other, dismissed him simultaneously from his post and her bed. Her next pupil, if rumour was to be believed, was a simple and jolly ploughboy. Since, indirectly, it was Mr Mellors who had set the seal on the amity between my Lord Chatterley and myself and had provided the instrument with which, not realizing it, Her Ladyship had blown my ship to harbour, I took pity on him, sad and uncouth creature that he was, and sent message that, if were lacking for fresh employment, he would be made welcome on our estates. He brought with him a mongrel cur that proved his inseparable companion; oft declaring of her that she was a bitch at once more affectionate, more obedient and less exacting than his former mistress.

Lucy and I now live in the greatest harmony and bliss, with our dear ones around us. Each month I make a brief sojourn of some three or four days in London, telling her that I must attend to business there. Though I am now so rich that I do not require the few sovereigns that this business brings to me, it is good for a married man to have some avocation. Absence from the beloved may make the heart grow fonder but abstinence from pleasure rarely does so. The chief guarantee of the continued happiness of our marriage is that I may regularly, if briefly, escape from it.

All that displeases me in my life is that, on occasion when I have been in London, I have overheard this or that gossip or slanderer refer to me maliciously as 'Lord Chatterley's Lover'. It is true that I have made love to many people and shall continue, God willing, to do so; but I have been and am the lover of Only One and so shall remain.

other novels by Francis King include:

A DOMESTIC ANIMAL

Antonio, a football-playing younger philosopher, visits England for research, leaving a wife and two children in Florence. With his general untidiness and lack of method he can hardly be called "a domestic animal", and the emotional and material poverty of his early life has left him with an unquenchable thirst for affection and admiration. But Dick Thompson, a successful middle-aged novelist with whom Antonio comes to stay, is more than willing to take care of his needs – for Dick has fallen in love with his handsome yet apparently heterosexual lodger.

"Francis King deserves the widest possible readership. He is a master-novelist" (Melvyn Bragg)

"A delicate and truly touching story" (*The Listener*)

"One of the most entertaining novels he has written. Entertainment, however, should not be confused with frivolity. Mr King has something deeply serious to say and if he says it readably, briefly and with dry humour, so much the better for the reader" (*Sunday Telegraph*)

ISBN 0 907040 32 2 (pbk)   UK £4.50/US $7.95
            34 9 (cased) UK £7.95/US $15.00

THE FIREWALKERS

First published in 1956, under the pseudonym "Frank Cauldwell", this accomplished comedy of manners is set among British expatriates and exotic locals in a Greece still undiscovered by tourism. Written with an infectious enjoyment and good humour, the story of the flamboyant and temperamental Colonel Theodore Grecos and his devotion to the completely unsophisticated Götz Joachim provides Francis King with ample scope for his mastery of ironic observation. In a new Introduction to this edition, the author explains how *The Firewalkers* came to be written, born of "the exhilarating sense of liberation that came to me on first setting foot in Athens".

"Astonishingly good. A witty and sympathetic writer who makes the most of his remarkable material, inventing characters and incidents with loving imaginative skill" (*Guardian*)

"Excellent. The author has the ability to be funny and moving at the same time, and his Theo and Gotz are two of the most engaging and human eccentrics I have met for a long time" (*Spectator*)

"Writes extremely well and holds our attention throughout not only delightfully but movingly". (*Times Literary Supplement*)

ISBN 0 907040 71 3 (pbk)   UK £4.95/US $7.50
         72 1 (cased) UK £9.95/US $18.95

THE MAN ON THE ROCK

Like many destitute and unemployed young men in post-war
Greece, Spiros Polymerides has only his natural cunning and good
looks to help him survive. As con-man, petty thief and parasite, he
moves relentlessly from victim to victim: Irvine, the repressed gay
man who befriends him; Helen, the wealthy, middle-aged English-
woman with whom he has an affair; Kiki, the Greek shipping heiress
he is eventually to marry. One by one he exploits and betrays them
all – only to discover that the final victim is himself.

"Reveals clearly Mr King's capacity for getting inside a character. In
this novel, he has succeeded not only in making a remarkably
understanding study of the relation between exploiter and ex-
ploited, but in presenting an extremely vivid picture of contempor-
ary Greece" (*Time and Tide*)

"Few English novelists have written with more might and assurance"
(*Spectator*)

ISBN 0 85449 022 1 (pbk) UK £3.95/US $7.95